NO TIME FOR APOLOGIES

NO BRIDES CLUB, BOOK 5

JEAN C GORDON

ISBN-13: 978-1-7321836-3-6

SWEET PROMISE PRESS
PO BOX 72
BRIGHTON, MI 48116

CHAPTER 1

K ate (or K.A. as the corporate name plate outside her cubicle at work read) Lewis stepped from the dimly lit stairwell into the still bright evening sun of the Briarwood Tavern's rooftop bar in the Tribeca neighborhood of New York City. She waved to her best friend Julie Harrison holding down their usual table, hitched her messenger bag up on her shoulder, and went straight for the antique mahogany bar.

"One fresh cherry margarita coming up," the regular Thursday evening bartender said when she reached her destination.

Kate eyed the glass the bartender lifted from the rack and flipped over with a twist of the wrist. "No, Andre, that won't do it tonight. Give me the monster size."

He looked at her straight on. "You know that's five times what you generally order."

"Yep, I did the math on the walk over."

"You've got it."

While she waited, Kate tapped her fingernails on the

1

wood and scanned the room, her gaze fixing on a guy sitting alone at a table for two, his eyes glued to his cell phone. Stood up? She blinked. The guy looked familiar, but she couldn't place him.

"Here you go." Andre slid her drink across the bar to her.

"Thanks." She cradled the glass in both palms and walked the table maze to where Julie was sitting.

"Well, are we celebrating?" Julie asked. "Did K.A. Lewis break the glass ceiling? Am I looking at the DeBakker Funds' new Growth and Income Fund Manager, the fund's first female manager?

"Not exactly." Kate sat, and took a healthy swallow of her drink.

"Want to spill or wait for the others? Julie asked.

Kate glanced toward the entrance. None of the other members of the No Brides Club had arrived yet. The group was her lifeline when she was drowning in frustration over her career. She didn't want to imagine what her life would be like without the support of other women who were equally focused on their careers. Women who were so focused that they'd decided not to weigh themselves down with the baggage of trying to balance romantic relationships on top of the struggle to climb the corporate ladder.

"No, I need to get it out." She was closest to Julie. They'd been friends since college. "But where is everyone, anyway?"

"Kinsley is upstate at her wildlife sanctuary, Rachel has an extra play practice, and Georgina and Melody are working late. So what excuse did your boss give you this round?"

Kate fortified herself with another slug of her margarita. It was the third time she'd been up for this promotion—a promotion she needed to take advantage of the opportunity she'd been offered recently to buy her apartment. Her apartment building was converting over to condos, and its location was too perfect to even think of moving. She'd earned this.

"Bob started with some BS about how I'd been putting in long hours lately, longer than usual, and my hard work had made a difference in our returns. I was on the edge of my chair, sure he was going to follow that up with an offer for the manager position."

"But, no." Julie shook her head, thumbs up, her mouth holding the O of no.

"No. The higher-ups want to delay naming a new manager." Kate slapped her palm to the table. "I was sure I had it this time."

"But you're still in contention?"

"Supposedly." Kate rested her elbows on the table and splayed her fingers, palms up. "I've paid my dues. Four years as a statistician and analyst for Growth and Income Fund, two of them as senior analyst, two years at a smaller fund family before that, and four years juggling that awful bank job and graduate courses for my MBA. What does it get me? A pat on the back, a small bonus next pay period, and an assistant for two months to help catch up on the backload of work the new software conversion caused."

"That rots."

"And that's not all. They've hired some guy who used to be an associate at the largest private equity firm in Boston as my assistant. No consulting me about it. Yeah, like a guy with those credentials wants to be an assistant statistician. Right." Kate gulped her margarita to the halfway mark. "So, I get to train the guy who'll probably get the manager position."

"What?" Julie placed her drink glass on the table with a clunk.

"Yep, first I asked Bob whether the guy seriously wanted to be an assistant statistician/analyst. I mean investment management is a cutthroat business. People don't take demotions, unless forced to."

"What did Bob say?"

Kate swirled her finger tip around the edge of her glass and licked the salt off. "He had the audacity to chuckle and say, 'No, he thinks he wants to be a professor at some small college upstate, but we'll convince him otherwise, eh.' You know, teamwork and all that."

Julie shook her head.

Kate downed most of the rest of her margarita to combat the bile rising in her throat. "Then I asked Bob outright if I was being asked to train this Smith guy ... his name is John Smith." Why did that name sound so familiar, other than it was terribly common? "Train the guy for the position I wanted." She cleared her throat. "Am I talking really loud?"

"No," Julie said. "Maybe a little. What was Bob's answer?"

Kate waved a hand at her friend. "He said I was still his first choice for the job, that the hiring came from higher up. His hands were tied." She leaned forward. "Well, I'm going to untie them. I don't care what John Smith's experience is. He's been hired as my assistant, and I'm not going to let him take my promotion."

"That's the spirit," Julie said. "I'm going to get a drink. You want another one?"

Kate eyed the empty monster glass. "I'll wait. I should eat something first."

Julie headed to the bar, and Kate's gaze followed her as far as the lone guy she'd spotted earlier. The bar server approached him and stood talking far longer than it would take her to get his drink order. She flipped her hair over her shoulder and said something that made the guy laugh. The server was flirting with him. Kate drew her lips into straight line. Not that there was any reason that should interest her. She was still focused on him after the server left and Julie returned.

"That *is* a nice view," Julie said before she sat.

"Hmmm?" Kate said.

"The eye candy sitting over there by himself."

"He looks so familiar, like I know him from somewhere," Kate answered as much to herself as to Julie.

"I TRUST your stay with us was enjoyable," The Greenwich Hotel concierge said as she opened the door for Jon Smith to exit.

"Excellent," he answered. It wasn't the Four Seasons, but had been more than fine for a one-night stay. Jon squinted at the bright sunlight that greeted him as he stepped outside. He was well-rested and ready for his meeting. Staying at the hotel had saved him the half hour to Rhinecliff and the two-hour early train to New York this morning. Getting up three-and-a-half hours before his meeting versus getting up an hour before should have been a no brainer. But it also entailed getting someone to stay with his grandfather, check on his livestock last night, and come feed them this morning.

Jon pulled open the gleaming glass doors to the DeBakker Mutual Funds office building, thinking he should be nervous, excited, *something* walking into his first face-to-face with a new employer. But he felt nothing but a little curious, maybe since he hadn't pursued the statistician position he was starting Monday. His former girlfriend Olivia had done that for him, before she'd thrown him over for a surgeon she'd met over coffee at the Westchester Medical Center when Grandpa had still been in inpatient rehabilitation there. Olivia had been staying at the farm with Jon then and had come to hospital with him.

He let the door drop closed behind him. Olivia had her father call a friend, who happened to be one of the DeBakkers of DeBakker Funds soon after Grandpa had had his stroke and Jon had moved from Boston to his grandfather's place. By the time he'd received the email setting up the Skype interview, she'd tired of what she called his playing at professor and gentlemen farmer. She'd needed a man she could depend on to keep her in the style Daddy had made her accustomed to. By then, Jon, as power of attorney for his grandfather after his stroke, had learned of the home equity loan Grandpa couldn't afford that he'd taken to come out of retirement and start up a grass-fed beef operation. The summer gig with DeBakker-Gelm would knock out a good chunk of that loan before Jon started his lower paying college instructor position in the fall.

His cell phone pinged as he pressed the elevator button for the fourth floor.

Morning. Thought I'd let you know I've made it to another day.

Grandpa and his gallows humor.

Good to know.

Jon stepped out into the hall.

Having breakfast with my babysitter.

He and his grandfather had gone 'round and 'round about Grandpa needing someone to stay with him, and Jon had finally gotten him to agree to the widow from up the road. Jon suspected his grandfather had a thing for Dottie—or at least he had before the stroke. Starting Monday, Dottie's 18-year-old grandson would be stopping in to do the chores and be there for Grandpa, and Dottie would be coming in the early evening to prepare supper.

Enjoy. I should be home about three.

Okay.

John checked the suite numbers on the offices for 410, where the funds' analysis and statistics offices were.

"Good morning," a young woman behind the reception desk greeted him. "How can I help you?"

"I'm Jon Smith. I have an appointment with Robert Conway."

"I'll let Bob know." She smiled, her gaze lingering on him a moment longer than he was comfortable with before she picked up her phone.

He still wasn't accustomed to the difference people—well, mostly women—saw in his appearance since he'd taken up swimming in college and dropped the extra 40 pounds he'd carried in high school. And he'd built up some muscle taking over for his grandfather on the farm.

"Jon." An affable man about Jon's father's age stepped into the reception area and offered his hand. "I'm Bob Conway."

After shaking hands, Bob said. "Leave your bag here with reception, and I'll take you up to HR to get all that out of the way first."

Jon handed the receptionist the gym bag he'd brought as his overnight bag and walked with Bob into the hall.

"Stairs good with you?" Bob asked, reaching for the knob to the stairwell door. "It's only two flights." He sized up Jon and patted his own slight paunch. "And I could use the exercise."

The old shame weighed his chest. "That's fine." Jon shoved his hands in his pockets while he waited for Bob to open the door.

"When you're done in HR," Bob said. "I'll introduce you to the senior statistician you'll be working with and the three of us can go to lunch."

"Sounds good." Jon grasped the handrail. That would shoot his plan to catch the 12:30 train and be home by three. He should still be home in time for afternoon chores. Grandpa had beef cattle now, not dairy, so the afternoon schedule wasn't as important, and their neighbor had said she'd stay as long as needed. Of course, Grandpa thought that was not at all. Jon made a mental note to phone Dottie first about the change in plans and then clue his grandfather in, so he didn't send her home.

An hour and a half later, after he'd filled out all the required papers, sat through an interactive video about corporate compliance, and completed the required computer modules on sexual harassment in the workplace and safety, Jon was back in the reception area of the statistics and analytics offices, sitting and waiting for Bob and the senior statistician to join him for lunch. He stood when he heard Bob's voice in the hall and looked in that direction. Bob walked toward him accompanied by a woman about Jon's age with brunette hair artfully pinned back from her attractive face. *Hmm.* Bob hadn't mentioned his new boss was a woman. Not that it mattered or that Bob should have.

As the pair stepped into the reception area, the office lighting played tricks with his eyes and superimposed an image of his high school secret crush and nemesis on the poised woman.

"Jon," Bob said, "this is ..."

Jon blinked. "Kate Lewis." The lighting hadn't been playing tricks.

"YOU TWO KNOW EACH OTHER, THEN," Bob said.

Kate stared. It was the man she'd seen at Briarwood last night, that Julie had referred to as eye candy. *It couldn't be. But it had to be. John/Jon Smith.* But this Jon Smith didn't look anything like her shy, pudgy classmate whom she hadn't been especially nice to. She cringed, trying to find her voice. She'd left that Kate back in Genesee when she'd headed off to college. She looked at the handsome, confident man standing in front of her. Evidently, Jon had left his high school self behind, too.

"We went to high school together," Jon filled the silence left by her surprise. "Good to see you, Kate."

She took his proffered hand and returned his firm handshake. "Good to see you, too." She meant that in the literal, not "let's relive the good old glory days" way. Who would have suspected those masculine high cheek bones lay beneath his formerly round cheeks? Not to mention the strong square jaw.

"Ah." Bob threw up his hands as if he'd made a grand discovery. "Then, you two don't need me. I'll leave you to catch up and order something in for myself. Take the afternoon if you'd like."

Kate fidgeted with the adjustable buckle on her bag's shoulder strap. She never fidgeted. She didn't want to spend the afternoon—let alone the next three months—with Jon, not after the way she and her friends had treated him. *Well.* Not only him, and not always. There were times when she and Jon had clicked in class, brought together by a shared, almost insane, fascination with numbers.

"After you." Jon held the office door for her.

"Thanks." As she stepped past him, she tried to recall him being so tall. Had he shot up after high school, or was it the change in his physique that had made her notice it?

"Where to?" Jon asked, standing close beside her on the crowded sidewalk.

Kate inched as far away as she could, to relieve the edginess of him being so close. While Kate loved being in the city, in the 10 years since she'd moved here permanently after earning her BA from NYU, she still wasn't used to all of the people. She chalked that up to her having lived 22 years outside Genesee in Western New York, nearly six hours from the city, where seeing ten people on the sidewalk in downtown at one time was a lot.

"The Briarwood Tavern has great sandwiches and salads."

"Sounds good to me. I stopped in there yesterday evening."

Kate weighed whether to mention she'd seen him. But that would remind him that she hadn't recognized him, and she needed a congenial work relationship that would allow her to assess Jon so she could put herself ahead of him in the race to portfolio manager. She studied his profile, wondering if he knew he was in the running yet.

"About the whole afternoon, what Bob said, I'd like to catch the 3:10 train to Rhinecliff, so I'm home for supper."

So, Jon didn't live in the metro area, would be commuting from one of the small towns up north, a ways up north. He probably had a family, which was almost as much of a career advantage to men as it was an obstacle to women.

"Can I say I'm relieved?" Kate cringed. That didn't come

out of her mouth right. Did she still harbor whatever it was that had always pressed her to get a dig in when she was with Jon?

Jon raised an eyebrow, an action that made his face even more stare-worthy than it already was.

"I have a lot of work on my desk and ..." She faltered. "And I keep feeling like I need to apologize for the way I treated you in high school."

"No need for apologies. You didn't treat me any differently than a lot of the other kids in our class, better than most of the ones in your group. Besides that was 15 years ago. We were kids."

Jon's easy acceptance didn't make her feel any less guilty.

"Have you kept in contact with anyone from high school?" Jon asked.

Maybe his acceptance wasn't so easy. Had he sensed her guilt and decided to play on it? She wasn't going to let him guilt her into giving him her promotion, if that was his plan. His open expression didn't give any hint of that.

"My first couple of years at NYU, I spent the summers at home, but once I'd escaped the family dairy farm and Genesee, I was a different person. Everyone I'd hung out with was still fixated on Genesee's football team being bumped out of the playoffs, where the next party was, and cutting down anyone who wasn't in our clique in high school." Kate pressed her lips together and felt her cheeks flush in embarrassment. She sure didn't sound any different than her old critical self. "How about you?"

"Dave Wheeler."

Another math-science nerd, Jon had hung around with. A dullness in her chest underscored that she hadn't been close enough to any of her high school friends for them or her to want to stay in contact.

"What's he up to?"

"He's a nuclear engineer out in California. I got together with him a couple of years ago when I was out there on business. Married. A couple of kids."

They reached Briarwood and Jon beat her to the door handle and held the dark wooden door open for her again.

The hostess approached them. "Are you here for lunch?" she asked before leading them to a corner table for two.

Kate pulled out her seat before Jon could, somehow needing to do that. "And you? Do you have a family?" She picked up the menu that she already knew by heart.

"Only if you count my grandfather as my kid, which is on mark a lot of the time. He had a stroke nine months ago. I left Boston to stay with him at his farm outside of Rhinecliffe, while he recuperated."

"That's why you left the private equity firm?" She placed her menu on the table.

"It was the excuse I needed to leave. While I love the mathematical challenges of financial management, I don't love the stress and cutthroat atmosphere of large financial services companies. Just give me some numbers to play around with and leave me to them, and I'm a happy camper." Jon grinned

Kate leaned back in her seat and tapped her splayed fingers to the table, remembering their shared love of math all through school and how in her quest for popularity in high school, she'd downplayed it with everyone but Jon.

"Then, as your boss, I have to ask you why are you working at DeBakker-Geld Funds?"

Their server interrupted to take their orders.

Once she'd left, Jon hesitated, unfolding his napkin before he answered, "To get some different experience before I start teaching in the fall."

He dropped his gaze to the napkin and flipped one corner repeatedly with his forefinger, making Kate suspect there was more to it than that. She wanted to take his answer at face value, believe that he wasn't a threat. But three years in the No Brides Club had taught her better, taught her to view any and all of her co-workers as competitors and to find the one chink in them that she could use in fortifying her wall against becoming too friendly with them.

"I'll be spearheading the new financial management program at Columbia-Greene, as well as teaching math."

Kate picked up her water glass, took a sip and placed the glass back on the table. "To be upfront, Bob dropped your hire on me unexpectedly. He mentioned your teaching, but I haven't even received your resume from HR yet. Have you been employed since you left the private equity group?"

One corner of his mouth twitched up before he answered. "Yes, I've been employed, although not in the financial services area."

He finished his answer with a full smile that made Kate marvel again at Jon's transformation since high school. His aura of confidence. His decisiveness. The clear delight on his face as he finished answering her question.

"I'm running a small herd of beef cattle on Grandpa's 200 acres, which is one of the reasons I need to catch the 3:10. I need to do evening chores."

Kate stared at him in his perfectly tailored suit and tried to imagine Jon as a farmer. She'd grown up on a farm, as had a fair number of her high school classmates. And at a young age had decided she would *not* live on a farm when she grew up. In contrast, Jon had lived in town. His parents were doctors at a medical center in Rochester.

She sized up his shoulders, then dropped her gaze to his hands. Although his nails were perfectly clipped, Jon's hands weren't the soft hands of a man who never got them dirty. Nor were his broad shoulders those of a white-collar professional—even one who worked out regularly. They were the hands of a working man. She could see him as a farmer. That was the chink in him she'd been looking for.

ate Lewis. That had been a surprise, and not an unpleasant one. Jon walked from the barn toward the house, chores done, his mind still on his day in the city. In his wildest thoughts, he couldn't have imagined that the K.A. Lewis in the directory listing HR had given him would turn out to be be his high school academic rival, sometimes nemesis, and major source of frustration for him through all four years. But that was all in the past. They were both different people now.

He shaded his eyes against the sun, and a picture of her sitting across from him at lunch, smiling at something he'd said flashed in his mind. He had to admit that he'd had good taste back then, even though he'd never pursued it. Kate had matured from a cute, albeit often stuck-up teen to a beautiful, poised, professional woman. He'd hold judgment on her personality until they'd worked together a while, although she'd been perfectly congenial at lunch. His neck prickled. They just had to co-exist as coworkers, colleagues. It wasn't as if he was looking for anything more from her. Kate wasn't his type. Nor was he looking at the job as anything more than the summer commitment he'd signed.

"Jon!" his grandfather bellowed from the back door of the house, blowing Jon's thoughts from his head.

"Coming." His grandfather's frustration at not being able to do everything he used to before the stroke made him impatient. Much more impatient than the man who'd let Jon trail after him asking incessant questions as a small child when he'd spent part of his summers with Grandpa and Grandma.

"I didn't hear you come in," Grandpa said when Jon reached the house.

"You were resting, and I didn't want to disturb you.

His grandfather eyed the t-shirt and jeans Jon had changed into. "I told Dottie to wake me if you weren't home when it was the time to do chores."

And Jon had told Dottie on the phone to let Grandpa be if he fell asleep. Jon had heard him rustle around his room numerous times last night.

Grandpa went inside. "I suppose you have everything done." He went down the list of things Jon had just completed.

"Yep," Jon answered to each. "Dottie said she left supper in the oven to keep warm."

Grandpa shuffled to his traditional seat at the head of the table while Jon carried the food dishes to the already set table.

"She's been cleaning again," the older man accused. "I can't find my bills or check book. It'll be May 1 on Monday. Things are due."

"They're covered. I still have the bills on automatic payment." He and his grandfather had had this conversation every month, since his stroke. And Grandpa always declined Jon's offer to stop the automatic payments.

"Not the barn loan. I always pay on that at the bank."

Jon followed his grandfather's gaze to the structure framed by the kitchen window. Being at the farm always gave Jon a sense of belonging, being part of a legacy. His mother's family, the Dutch Meijers, who'd become Meyers, had farmed this land for more than 370 years. He clenched his jaw. And his mother didn't care at all about that. She wanted Grandpa to sell the farm and move to some kind of assisted living facility for seniors.

"You're good. I already paid what's due for May…" and a good share more … "when I was in town earlier this week checking on the deposit from the stock I sold." Most of the home equity loan Grandpa had taken before his stroke had gone toward replacing the old dairy barn with a more modern design for grazed beef cattle. Although Jon nostalgically missed the old red barn of his childhood, the new barn was state-of-the-art, exactly what they needed for the beef operation.

He lifted the lid off the skillet of fried chicken Dottie had made and breathed in the enticing smell. If things went as he planned, he should have the loan mostly paid off by the end of his work at DeBakker and Grandpa talked into letting him pay half of the payments after that as part of their partnership agreement.

"Let's dig in."

"Harrumph." His grandfather speared a drumstick with the serving fork. "I still need my checkbook."

"I'll help you look for it after we finish eating." Jon scooped a healthy serving of mashed potatoes onto his plate, but not without the familiar twinge of shame from his mother's admonishments to watch his carbs when he was growing up—and out. "You'll never guess who my new boss is."

"How should I know?" Grandpa lost control of his fork, and it clattered to his plate. "I don't know anyone in New York," he grumped.

Jon's chest tightened. "Kate Lewis. From Genesee." He didn't expect his grandfather to remember her, but it turned the conversation away from his grandfather's finances and stroke-related limitations.

Grandpa grinned. "The little girl you used to complain about all the time?"

Kate certainly wasn't a little girl anymore. She was all woman.

"I wasn't sure you'd remember her." Once again, his grandfather had surprised him with his sharpness and memory.

"How could I forget?"

Jon uncrossed and re-crossed his ankles under the table. Grandpa was probably remembering him as the brat who showed up on his doorstep shortly after high school graduation angry with his parents, himself, and the world at large. Jon flinched inwardly. He'd blamed Kate for getting "his" math scholarship. That award would have allowed him to pay his own way through college, with the help of limited student loans, so that he could major in math rather than pre-med as his parents insisted, if they were paying.

"The summer after graduation?" Jon asked. He'd been such an idiot to blame Kate when his anger was fueled by his immaturity and family problems.

"When you came here and went to Columbia-Greene for your first year of college? Nah. I was thinking back to when you were in first or second grade and you announced to any and everyone who would listen that you'd found the girl you were going to marry. That she was good in math and loved numbers as much as you did."

"I said that?"

"You sure did. Pass me some more of those potatoes."

Jon smiled, imagining Kate's expression if he told her about his elementary school plan to marry her. He'd done his best to keep any romantic interest he might have had in her well- hidden once they'd hit middle school, as much to keep the guys from mocking him as to avoid her scorn if she'd found out.

"What are you grinning at?" his grandfather asked.

Jon told him.

"You didn't ask for my advice, but that's a bad idea,"

Jon had to refrain from chuckling at his grandfather's earnestness. "I wouldn't mention it. She's my boss, and we'll only be working together for a couple of months. I don't expect to become that friendly. We weren't close in high school. Dotty makes great fried chicken, doesn't she?"

Grandpa grunted and Jon concentrated his attention on his nearly untouched supper to move his mind off Kate and the possibility of becoming friendly. *Still. There'd been times.* In middle school, the couple of summers when they'd both gone to a month-long math camp at Rochester Institute of Technology. His parents had driven them, since they went into Rochester for work. He and Kate had been friends for the duration of camp, at least. The same when they'd competed in the Mathletes competition in Syracuse as members from the Genesee County team.

He dug into his chicken without really tasting it. Even at college, among his fellow math majors, he hadn't run into any girls ... women... who found the joy in math that Kate had. Rather than their minds clicking as his and Kate's had, he'd come away from the few romantic relationships he'd had with college classmates feeling as if he'd been through some kind of competition of the minds.

Jon swallowed his mouthful of chicken. His former feelings for Kate had been an unrequited juvenile crush. She was his boss. It wasn't as if he was contemplating any relationship with her, other than work. He scooped up a forkful of potato he didn't want. So why couldn't he stop thinking and talking about her?

KATE HIT the DeBakker-Gelm offices 15 minutes earlier than usual. She wanted time to center herself before she had to begin the day with her new assistant. She swiped her employee card and flung open the plate glass door. She'd thought she'd left Genesee and small-town life behind her years ago. Jon brought it all back.

The shade of the awning highlighted her reflection in the glass and her already creased pants. Why had she worn linen, knowing how it wrinkled? Kate frowned. The bigger question was why did she care? If a man looked rumpled, it was generally assumed he was working hard. She didn't have any greater need to impress anyone today than any other work day.

"Good morning," a familiar deep voice said behind her.

She let out a startled, "Yip."

Jon caught the door she'd lost her grip on.

"You startled me." Kate took in his cool, calm, and collected appearance. He could be an ad for Armani, although she had no idea what suit he was wearing. *No.* She had no need to impress anyone, but she couldn't deny it. She had a want. A want she shouldn't have. Jon was her assistant. She didn't need to impress him with anything, except the fact that she was in charge. It was action not appearance that would do that.

"Sorry." He placed one foot across the door threshold.

"Wait." Her tone made the word sound like a command.

He stopped and looked around. "What?"

"It's company policy not to let co-workers in on your employee card. For security reasons, we like to know who's in the building."

His lips quirked up in a smile that brought out faint laugh lines at the corners of his eyes. "I haven't even officially started my first day and I'm already in trouble with the boss." Jon stepped back, let the door close, and pulled his employee card from his wallet.

The flush that colored Kate's cheeks had nothing to do with the heat of her walk to work. Juvenile expressions of power weren't going to win Jon's professional respect, nor particularly earn her points with Bob. She waited while Jon swiped his card and reentered, still smiling. She dropped her gaze to avoid his, and it fixed on the bag in his left hand. Did he always carry a gym bag?

He raised the bag slightly. "I hope to make swim practice on the way home."

"Oh, you coach kids?" A twinge of jealousy pricked Kate. With all the time she put in at the office, she barely had time for the No Brides on Thursdays, let alone any other social or volunteer activities.

"No, I swim competitively with the US Masters Hudson Dolphins."

Kate lifted her gaze. That would explain his physique. That and daily chores. She sucked in her stomach and tried to remember the last time she'd hit the yoga studio. "You didn't swim in high school."

"I did, but not on the swim team. I got interested in competitive swimming at college."

She allowed herself one more glance. If Jon had swum in high school, maybe she would have been interested. She turned her focus to the bank of elevators in the lobby. *Nah,* probably not. He still would have been a math nerd, and in her teenage immaturity, she'd worked hard at downplaying how smart she was to fit in with the popular crowd, while still earning the grades she needed to get more of her college paid for with scholarships and grants. Besides, her former shallow self would have categorized swimming as a minor sport. At their hometown school, football was king and basketball a far second, with any other sports also-rans. Still if Jon had looked like he did now back then ..."

"Then, I flew up and made my landing on the top deck of the Empire State Building."

Kate's forefinger stopped a half inch short of the elevator up button. "Pardon?"

"Ah, you were lost in thought."

"I'm afraid I was. I'm usually one of the few people here this early. I organize my day on the walk over and up to my cubicle." That was true. She pressed the button. She didn't say that's what she was thinking about now. "You were saying something about the Empire State Building."

"To get your attention." He motioned for her to step into the elevator ahead of him.

He'd had her attention all right. Just not what he was saying.

"I was wondering about my office. Bob was going to show me after lunch, but he didn't have lunch with us and I headed right to Penn Station afterwards."

There was one empty office in the analytics suite. But she had a cubical, albeit a cubical on a windowed wall. Bob couldn't possibly be giving her assistant his own office on orders from above to entice Jon to stay. The thought sucker-punched her.

Jon reached past her to press the fourth-floor button, which gave her a moment to collect her thoughts. One of the things she'd been planning to do first thing this morning before Jon arrived was to check her email for info on where Jon would be working, something she should have checked with HR Friday, since Bob had been out of the office.

She quietly sucked in a deep breath. Scattered was not an adjective people would be prone to use to describe her. Her phone pinged, and Kate pulled it from the pocket of her elbow-sleeved shrug. A glance at the screen showed a low balance text from her bank. She tilted the screen away from Jon and pressed her email app to see if there was an email from either Bob or HR about where she should put Jon. There was. The relief made her almost giddy. Or it could have been the close quarters of the elevator. She welcomed the whoosh of fresh air when the elevator doors opened and she stepped into the hall.

"Come on, I'll show you your work space. HR probably told you that the analysts and statisticians and our staff work in an open access layout to facilitate working together."

The left side of his mouth curved up. "In other words, cubicles. I got the tour Thursday."

"Exactly. You're here." Kate pointed at a workspace across from the open side of hers, without a window. "Get yourself settled and I'll go over the Growth and Income Fund's open projects you'll be working on,"

"Copy that."

Kate crossed the walkway between their cubicles and, out of sight behind the partition, sank into her Hon chair, a perk she'd gotten with her last promotion to senior statistician.

The US financial markets didn't open for nearly an hour and a half, yet she felt like she'd put in a whole day already. If she didn't get a grip on the situation fast, the fund manager promotion wouldn't matter. She'd be burned to a crisp long before the time the decision was made.

JON REMOVED his leather briefcase from his gym bag and placed it on the small side table connected to the computer stand before he stashed the bag under the table. He surveyed his work area. It was a far cry from the office he'd had at the private equity firm. But most people would say his position was a big comedown, as well. He flipped open his company laptop and pressed the on button. Not him. His purpose wasn't to make his mark at DeBakker-Gelm. Jon opened his briefcase and took out the personalized employee handbook he'd received Thursday, flipped it open for his company username and password.

Nope. All he was looking for was extra income this summer to knock off his grandfather's home equity loan and the possibility of some part-time mid-level remote work to supplement his community college instructor's salary the rest of the year.

Working with Kate was a bonus. He was familiar with her intelligence, and her expertise could give him the knowledge he wanted to keep a hand in the investment sector while he taught. She wouldn't hold the position she did at the fund if she didn't know what she was doing. And her appearance certainly brightened up the drab office space, although he knew appearances could be deceiving.

He watched the computer's desktop icons load. It was a fact, that he had little trouble attracting women, beautiful women, and enjoying his time with them until he, usually, lost interest in them.

What was he doing, mixing thoughts of Kate, beautiful women, and relationships? This was work. Besides, he'd seen with his parents what happened in a relationship when two great minds bonded. Bickering, competition, battles for control, and no time or feelings for anyone else. An emptiness he hadn't experienced in a long time hollowed out his insides. He clicked the email icon, set up his account on the computer and read the canned welcoming email from HR. Then he set up the account on his phone.

Jon stood. That was about the extent of his settling. *Time to get to work.* A new email alert flashed on the computer screen. A second email from HR joined the welcome. He clicked and read the message.

Bob thought you might be interested.

Interested in what? He clicked the attachment and scratched his head. It was a job announcement about a portfolio manager position. What was there about the position that he couldn't read between the lines, that Bob would have HR send it to ... Jon glanced at the computer clock ... someone who hadn't been working here not quite a half-hour yet? In the usual job progression, one of the analysts or statisticians would be tapped for the position.

The squeak of the wheels on Kate's chair sounded across the walkway between their cubicles and a buzz of humor ran through Jon. *The squeaky wheel gets the grease.* Kate always had been the squeaky wheel. Not that he was interested in the position, but if there wasn't something negative about the Growth and Income Fund, Kate would surely have the job. In three steps he was at Kate's cubicle, which he noticed had a window view.

"I'm ready to get started."

Kate clicked shut whatever she'd been working on, and he reflexively shifted his weight back on his heels. He wouldn't have pegged Kate as the type of co-worker who hoarded information. But maybe that was the culture here. He hoped not. That could make his tenure here a very long couple of months. Or she might have been doing something nonwork that was none of his business. *Yeah.* He'd go with the last one.

"Okay, if Bob didn't introduce you around, let's start here. Staff should be arriving."

"Sounds good. The only introductions Bob did were HR and you."

"Then, we'll start with the front desk."

As Kate slipped by him to exit her cubical, he caught a scent that reminded him of the sugar cookies his grand-mother used to make him. He sure loved those cookies. Jon shook the memory from his head. *Work. You're at work.*

"Follow me." Kate crooked a finger at him.

Jon held back the quip, *I'd follow you anywhere* and walked beside her.

"For the most part, my research is for the company's Balanced and Growth and Income Funds."

All-business Kate pulled him back into the world of work and rekindled his curiosity about the email he'd received. "I got a strange email about one of the funds from HR, just now, when I finished setting up my email."

Kate stopped, hands on hips. "You sure it was from HR and not one of the fund managers trying to grab you for a project, rather than putting in an official request?"

"It was definitely from HR. An interoffice announcement about an open portfolio manager position."

Kate's stride faltered, and he reached over to take her elbow, pulling back when she steadied herself.

"What's so toxic about the Growth and Income Fund that the company would try to pawn it off on a new employee."

"Not. A. Thing."

Jon cocked his head and studied the range of emotions Kate was fighting to keep out of her expression. "I figured if you hadn't taken the move up, there must be a good reason for not taking it."

Instead of filling him in with more, Kate grabbed the arm of a 20-something-looking guy walking past. "Scott, this is my new assistant Jon Smith. Scott is an analyst."

The two men shook hands.

"Could you finish taking Jon around to meet everyone? I've got to go talk with Bob."

"Sure," Scott said.

Jon watched Kate storm away. He wouldn't want to be Bob right now.

"What's that all about?"

"The squeaky wheel getting some grease," Jon muttered.

"Pardon?" Scott asked, his gaze following Jon's.

"Nothing."

But it was something. Kate turned a corner out of view. A big something, he'd say. One that he needed to pin down if he was going to get the most out of his time here.

CHAPTER 3

But you're only a girl.

Kate shuffled the pages on her desk. Where had her older brother's childhood taunt come from? Other than her boss Bob being in meetings every time she'd tried to connect with him, her first day with Jon had gone okay. She wasn't at all surprised Jon had been a quick study and by afternoon was able to take on a research request on his own, albeit a pretty simple one. He'd probably done similar research at the equity firm—and a lot more. But she was the one in charge here, and it was her prerogative to give him the grunt work, if she so chose. Besides Jon had seemed sincere in wanting to stay at DeBakker-Gelm for only the summer. He'd expressed a curiosity about the Growth and Income Fund manager position, but hadn't seemed interested in it.

She'd thought she'd finally buried her brother Josh's childhood digs, and her father's less blatant sexism—despite his pride in her accomplishments—when she'd landed the analyst job with DeBakker. Kate killed the insecurity that had bubbled up, threatening to break through the barrier she'd built against it and walked over to Jon's cubical.

"Shouldn't you get going to make your train?

"Throwing me out, are you?"

Kate wanted to disappear back into her cubicle and start over again, after she completely stomped down her old insecurities. What was with her? She *did* want him to leave because she was more than ready to go herself but reluctant to do so before him. Was it the high school connection? That was so juvenile.

"No, you mentioned this morning wanting to make your swim practice."

Jon shrugged. "No big deal." He motioned to his computer. "I have one thing I want to finish. I should still be able to make the train."

"Okay. No need to stay late your first day. You'll have plenty of opportunities to later."

"Got it." He drew an air checkmark. "Finish quickly and get out while I can. But plan to camp out here in the future." He grinned, which for whatever reason, cleared some of the emotional fog that had her reverting to adolescence.

Kate laughed. "Just finish your work and have a good evening."

"You, too."

He turned back to the computer and she made a final pass by Bob's office to see if he was still in. He rarely left before six. His office door was half open and the light still on. She knocked on the door and walked in.

"Kate." He looked up from the papers he was reading.

"Are you avoiding me?" she asked.

"Not at all. I just sent you an email, figured you'd be gone home."

Kate pulled a chair over. "Seriously? When was the last time you saw me out of her before six?"

"Last Thursday."

Kate gritted her teeth. He was going to be like that? "What's with HR sending my assistant the announcement about the portfolio manager position?" She sat before the steel in her backbone softened.

"That direction came from above."

Again, from above. She steeled herself. What did it matter? If she didn't get the promotion this time, she was out of here. "Okay. Be straight with me. Am I still in the running for manager?"

Bob's posture relaxed. "Definitely, and you're still my first choice. Humor the big guys."

Kate rose. "I'm not going to humor anyone. I'm going to make sure there's no question that I'm the person DeBakker needs to manage the Growth and Income Fund."

Not waiting for a response, she turned on her heel and walked back to her cubicle, shaking in a combination of fury and "what have I done?"

Halfway there, her cell phone rang. *Bob?* She glanced at the screen. Her 21-year-old sister Ava.

"Hey squirt." Kate worked at making her greeting sound upbeat. "To what do I owe the honor of you calling instead of texting?"

"It's a surprise. Mom and Dad don't know. Trey and I are engaged."

Kate searched for the right words and went for humor. "Etiquette says I'm not supposed to congratulate a woman on her engagement, so what do I say?"

"Say you're happy for me."

"I am happy for you." Kate had nothing against marriage —for other people. Ava and Trey had been dating since

Ava's senior year in high school. And Ava was finishing up her associate's degree in early childhood education with a job waiting for her with the Genesee Central School District's Pre-K program.

Ava's voice flattened. "I'm not sure Mom and Dad will be. You and Josh are hard acts to follow. Mom and Dad only have associate's degrees. Why do they think I need a BA in education?"

Kate laughed.

"It's not funny," Ava protested.

"No, it's not. It's ironic. You were too little to know, but Mom and Dad couldn't understand why I needed a master's degree."

"That's when you moved to New York permanently."

"Maybe you weren't too little."

"I'm so glad you're going to be here when I tell them, after the graduation ceremony."

Oh, no. Kate gripped her phone. That was *this* weekend. With Jon's appearance on the scene, she'd forgotten all about Ava's graduation and party and the vacation days she'd scheduled for Friday and Monday.

"My graduation. You didn't forget, did you?"

Guilt consumed Kate. "Forget my baby sister's college graduation. Of course not."

"Text me when you'll be getting in Friday, and I'll come pick you up at the Rochester Amtrak station. We'll have a girls' dinner out before we go back to the house, talk about maid of honor dresses."

"Sweetie, you want me to be your maid of honor?" Kate's heart swelled, obliterating the efforts of her conscience to remind her of all the times she hadn't been there for Ava.

"Who else?"

"You've got it. Love you."

"Love you."

Two days away from work, with her new assistant barely on the job. Kate was surprised that Bob hadn't asked her to change her time off. A lead weight dropped into the pit of her empty stomach. Two days with Jon reporting to Bob. Two days with her not in the office running interference between Jon and Bob and the powers that be.

For a fleeting moment, Kate calculated the possibility of getting a train early enough Saturday to make Ava's graduation ceremony at Genesee Community College in Batavia. She shook her head. That wouldn't be fair to Ava. She'd be breaking another promise to her. Kate sensed rather than saw someone approaching her in the narrow walkway.

"Good. I caught you. I thought you might have left," Jon said.

There was no reason his words should have lifted her spirits. But they did a bit. "I was talking with Bob." She studied Jon for a reaction. After all, she wasn't 100% certain he didn't want the manager position.

He shifted from foot to foot, and the lead in her stomach increased. What did he not want to tell her?

"I, uh, hate to ask since I've just started here. But could I take off Friday?"

Half the lead melted.

"Sort of a family emergency."

"Your grandfather?"

"No, my father had surgery and will be coming home Friday. They thought it would be Monday, and the nursing service they scheduled isn't starting until then. He's having trouble with a reaction to the pain meds. My mother doesn't think she can handle him on her own, even for a couple of days. Besides, she has some big charity thing going on this weekend that she *can't miss*."

The lack of any warmth in Jon's tone wasn't lost on Kate. She knew he wasn't close to his parents, or hadn't been when she knew him before.

"Yeah, I'm their last resort," he said as if reading her thoughts. "After all, it's not like I'd have anything important to be doing." Jon rolled his eyes.

The rest of the lead evaporated. "Actually, I'm taking off Friday and Monday for my sister's college graduation. You can do the same."

"Thanks. How are you getting up to Genesee?"

"Train."

"If you don't have your ticket yet, let me give you a lift there and back."

Five hours in close quarters with Jon. There and back. Confident. Handsome. Funny. And oh so smart Jon, who was and wasn't the same boy who'd been around the edges of her life for 13 years.

Despite all efforts on her part, her pulse ticked up and her throat tightened.

JON PULLED his car into the Hudson Amtrak station parking lot, air conditioning blasting against the incredibly warm late-May morning temperature. He smiled as his mind replayed the myriad of expressions that had passed over Kate's face before she'd agreed to take him up on his offer. She'd insisted on taking the train to the station north of the farm so he wouldn't have to go out of his way to pick her up. Then, he'd hardly had contact with her for the rest of the week, although she'd kept him busy with projects dropped in his in-box outside his cubicle or with various analysts.

"The Maple Leaf from New York continuing to Albany,

Schenectady, and points west is arriving on track ...” The public address system announced Kate's train as Jon walked into the station. He looked up at the clock. 8:45, right on time. He looked over the few people entering the station from the track. No Kate. Although he hadn't heard his phone's text alert, he checked the phone anyway. Nothing there. She would have had to catch the train at the crack of dawn. Had she fallen asleep on the ride here? He continued toward the trackside doors, unable to quell a weird feeling that he'd been stood up, like this was a date or something.

At the doorway, he shielded his eyes from the sun with his hand and looked out. *There she was*. His breath left him. What was that about? He dropped his hand as Kate walked down a step, stood, and looked up into the train. Her casual jeans and t-shirt made her look softer, younger than she did in her dress-for-success business clothes. More like she had when he'd crushed on her at school. His heart flip-flopped in an adolescent repeat of the state he'd been in for much of his teens.

An elderly woman appeared in the doorway. Kate descended another step and reached up to take the woman's bag in one hand and offer her other arm to the woman, who took Kate's elbow and slowly stepped down. They repeated the action and the older woman made her way to the platform. Jon warmed at Kate's thoughtfulness.

“Excuse me,” a thin voice said behind him.

Jon walked out to make way for a frail looking man with a walker.

The elderly woman waved.

“That's my girl,” the elderly man said. “She's been downstate visiting our new great-granddaughter. “Since they appear to be the last ones off, I take it the other girl's yours?”

“Yes, I mean, that's Kate.” Jon stumbled on his words.

"I'm here to pick her up. From the train. I'll go help with their bags." He closed the distance to the women in a few strides before he made a complete buffoon of himself.

"I'll take those." Jon reached for the bags.

"You must be Jon, the older woman said as she handed him hers. "Kate told me all about you. You are a handsome one."

"Thank you." Jon preened at the thought of Kate talking about him, possibly about his appearance. Maybe she was attracted to him. He roadblocked that out-of-control train with the silent reminder, *she's your boss.*

"Yes," the woman continued. "Kate told me all about how you knew each other in high school and how you met again recently at work when she found out she was your new boss." The woman chuckled. "Things are sure different today, and for the better." Her eyes twinkled as she tipped her head toward Jon. "I never had such a nice view at any of the jobs I had when I was young."

"Edna, you crack me up," Kate said, nodding

Jon dropped his gaze to the train platform. *Eye candy.* Guess that put him in his place. But that's usually where he wanted to be with women—casual, no strings attached. So he didn't know why Kate's nod felt like a gut kick.

"Ralph." Edna looked over Jon's shoulder. "Excuse me." She walked around Jon to the man with the walker and shared a kiss. "You didn't have to come out to meet me."

"Yes, I did. I couldn't wait to see you."

The older woman's blush warmed Jon.

"And I'll take that bag," Ralph said.

"I've got it." Jon took in the wheels on the walker and the expression on the other man's face. "Right here," he finished, handing the bag over so Ralph could wrap his hand around the handle and his walker at the same time.

"It was nice meeting you, Kate," Edna said as she turned to leave.

"The same here."

"I'll email you that information about my Tai Chi class."

"I'll be looking for it."

Jon watched the older couple walk away, her arm resting on his waist. Sadness enveloped him. Was that generation, his grandparents' generation, the last to master happily ever after in a relationship? He certainly hadn't seen it with his parents or many of his friends' parents. As for himself, he hadn't ever gotten past superficial to even think about a future with anyone.

"They're adorable, aren't they?" Kate asked.

"I guess." He shrugged, ridding himself of any lingering envy of what he saw in the elderly couple.

Kate's eyes softened. "I can see my parents like them in 25 years."

"Really?" Jon couldn't contain his surprise

"Sure, now that they don't have kids hanging on them, they hold hands when they walk together, kiss before one of them leaves the house. And with Dad moving toward 60, Mom fusses over him, worries about him doing too much around the farm, not letting his part-time hand and the teenager he hired in the summer and after school do enough. Dad still brings her little bouquets of wild violets and daisies when he finds them.

The light Kate's smile brought to her eyes made him want to be where she was, in the happy place her observations had taken her.

"Sometimes I think they're heading into their second childhood." She laughed. "How about you, your parents?"

Jon swallowed against the desert in his throat before he spoke. He didn't want his envy and lack of any real relationship with his parents to show. "I don't see them often. Their busy schedules, Grandpa, the livestock." The more he said, the lamer he sounded.

"But when they needed you, asked for your help this weekend, you were ready to go."

Jon didn't want to correct Kate. His mother didn't ask, she commanded. And he was going to Genesee for Grandpa, not his mother or father. The old guy fought letting on how hurt he was that his only daughter, only child was estranged from him. Jon and his parents didn't get along well, but Jon talked to them when they called and answered their emails.

"You know who Edna and Ralph remind me of?" Jon altered the conversation path.

"Who?"

"My grandma and grandpa before Grandma died." Jon blinked against the sun. Without being aware, he and Kate had walked through the small train station and out the other side by the parking lot. "My car's the green Forester."

"Not a Mercedes or Beamer? I thought all you financial types drove them."

Jon squirmed. He had had a BMW when he was in Boston. "Not so handy on the farm."

A frown Jon couldn't read flitted across Kate's face before she recovered with, "True. Are you telling me I should be glad it's not a 1998 Ford 150?"

"Your dad still has it?" Jon asked. Kate had always been embarrassed when her father picked her up from Mathletes practice in his farm pickup, not that other teammates didn't have parents driving pickups.

"He does. He couldn't bear to trade it in on his new one."

Jon opened the trunk and put Kate's bag in before opening the passenger side door for her. This was good. All he needed to do was keep her talking about her family, friends, anything but him and his family.

Jon pressed the starter and then the gas, watching Kate from the corner of his eye as she settled in

"So," she said once she appeared to be comfortable, "what were you saying about your grandparents?"

AFTER EXHAUSTING small talk about Jon's grandparents, her siblings, work, and the weather, Kate leaned back in her seat, closed her eyes, and enjoyed the warm morning sun on her face while she listened to the music Jon had put on. Classic jazz, something they had in common besides math.

"Hey."

A motion to her left made Kate jerk upright and glance around. They were on her parents' road. She'd fallen asleep. Her cheeks flushed with heat that had nothing to do with the sun. She looked at the dashboard clock. She'd been asleep for the past hour with her head leaning toward Jon and her arm resting on the console touching Jon's thigh.

Kate smoothed her hair. "Sorry, I wasn't much company for you on the drive."

"No problem."

Was that a tinge of pink on his cheeks, or was she projecting her embarrassment onto him? "It's the next driveway."

"I know." He flicked the directional and pulled in.

How did Jon know? Before Kate could dissect that bit of information, Ava came bounding out of the house to the car as if she were 10 not 20.

Ava pulled open the passenger-side door as soon as Jon stopped.

"You're here. I thought you were going to text me when you reached Batavia."

"Um, I fell asleep sometime before Rochester."

Ava grabbed her hand and pulled her out for a hug. "If you're not driving, you always fall asleep in the car. You should have warned ..." She released Kate motioning toward Jon, who'd gotten out and was walking to the back hatch to get Kate's suitcase.

"Ava, this is Jon Smith. You'd be too young to remember, but Jon and I went to high school together. We recently ran into each other in the city."

"Hi, Ava," Jon said with a smile that made Kate's stomach lurch. "You must be the toddler in the car seat who came along for the ride when your father drove Kate and me to Mathletes competitions."

"That would be me." Ava returned Jon's smile.

Kate stared at Ava. Her sister wasn't flirting with Jon, was she? Not that Jon wasn't flirt-worthy. That is, under the right circumstances. Which this wasn't.

Jon closed the back door and joined them on their side of the car. Kate reached for her bag.

He held on to it for an extra couple of seconds. "I'll see you Monday. Text me when you're ready to go."

"Don't you want to come in and say hi to Mom and Dad?" Ava asked, donning their mother's *where are your manners expression.*

"Yes, I'm sure they'd love to see you again." Kate pulled up the suitcase handle to roll it to the house and hoped her invitation didn't sound as forced to Jon as it did to her.

"So," Ava said, "Where did you two run into each other?"

"At work," Jon answered. "Kate's my boss."

"Get out!" Ava squealed, sizing up Jon before looking at Kate. "Then, you're not ... together."

"You'll have to excuse Ava. She's recently en—" Ava's glare stopped Kate from blabbing her sister's private news. "She's happily in a relationship and wants to include everyone in her bliss." Kate cringed. That wasn't any better than breaking her sister's confidence. Why was she being so catty to Ava?

The door to the kitchen swung open and Kate's mother greeted them. "Jon, come in. Thanks for giving Kate a ride. I almost wouldn't have recognized you all grown up."

"Hi, Mrs. Lewis."

Kate caught Jon's squirm out of the corner of her eye, along with the flash of relief on his face when his cell phone dinged.

"Sorry. It's my grandfather. He doesn't call unless he has a reason."

"Of course," Kate's mother said. "Take your call, Jon, and then join us in the kitchen."

Kate and Ava slipped by and into the house

Their mother hugged Kate and then held her out at arm's length, smiling. "How did you run into Jon? You didn't say in your text."

"Wait until you hear," Ava said before Kate could answer.

Her mother released her. "Sit and have some iced tea and talk. Your dad should be in soon. You can take your bag up to your room after Jon leaves."

Kate glanced back out the kitchen window at Jon smiling at his phone. His grandfather must be okay. Jon lifted his head and their gazes locked long enough for her stomach to flip-flop before she broke the connection. It must be relief that nothing was wrong.

"Are you hungry?" Mom asked as she placed the pitcher

of iced tea on the table. I have a package of those `Nutter Butter cookies you always liked."

Hunger. Of course. That's why her stomach had spasmed like that when Jon looked at her.

"Or I can make you and Jon sandwiches."

"None for me, thanks." Jon walked in. "I need to get to my parents' house."

Good. Jon wasn't any more anxious to stay than she was to have him stay.

"You can have a glass of tea, can't you?" her mother asked. "Paul will be right in. Kate was about to tell us how you two ran into each other." She moved one of the tumblers from the middle of the table to the seat next to Kate.

"I can stay a few minutes."

Jon's leg brushed hers as he took his seat. Kate cleared her throat. "We met at work. Jon is working with my group for the summer."

Ava plopped into the seat across from them and glanced from her to Jon. "But that's not the good part. Kate is Jon's boss."

Kate's mother pursed her lips. "Small world."

Kate knew her mother was proud of her. She also knew Mom was uncomfortable with her living in New York City and her dedication to her career.

"Yes," Jon said. "I'm Kate's assistant. She's showing me the ropes, for a financial planning course I'll be teaching at Columbia-Greene Community College."

While she didn't need Jon's help with her mother, she had to admit that she didn't mind him jumping in to run interference. She poured Jon and herself a glass of tea. "Your grandfather's okay? Your phone call?"

"Oh, yeah. It was good news. One of our cows had twin heifers after I left this morning."

They all looked toward the door as Kate's father joined them.

"Hi, Jon, good to see you," he said

"You, too, Mr. Lewis." Jon stood and the two men shook hands.

"I overheard. Your grandfather is still running his dairy farm?"

"No, we're running beef cattle. A joint operation."

Her father wanted all the details.

Before Jon got started on those details, Kate said. "I'll text you Sunday morning about the drive home."

"Sure thing," Jon answered.

As Jon dived back into his conversation with her dad, Kate excused herself to head upstairs to check her work email—and to avoid any circling back of the conversation to her and Jon.

Kate hadn't realized how on edge she'd been until she felt her uneasiness lifting with each step she took toward her childhood room. Two and a half days away from the office. Away from Jon.

CHAPTER 4

*J*on didn't often do stupid things. But he just had. He'd been so comfortable sitting at the Lewis's kitchen table, drinking Mrs. Lewis's tea and eating the sandwich she'd made for him. Talking cattle-raising with Mr. Lewis. Putting off going to his parents' place. When he'd finally risen to leave and Kate's sister Ava had invited him to her graduation party Saturday afternoon, it had been so easy to say "yes." Kate's mother had added that his parents were welcome to come as well.

A horn honked, and a quarter of the way into the inter-section, he slammed on the brakes for the stop sign at the corner of the Lewis' road and the highway into the Village of Genesee. The driver of the car on the highway shouted something at him that was muted by the closed windows in each car. But Jon could fill in the words. Gripping the steering wheel and breathing deeply to slow his pounding heart, he made his right turn. What was with him, that he'd been *that* lost in thought? One word lashed in his mind: *Kate. No.* He wasn't a love-sick, hormone-driven adolescent anymore. It had to be the prospect of several days with his parents.

Another car passed him, and he glanced at the speedometer. Forty-five in a 55-mile-per-hour zone. He was doing it again. Jon pressed the accelerator and blanked his mind to anything but his driving until he reached his parents' home on the outskirts of Genesee. Before getting out of the car, he stared at the house he'd grown up in. It was a similar style to the Lewis' farmhouse, except that it wasn't a typical nineteenth century Upstate New York farmhouse. It was a 1980s replica of one. No detail had been spared, right down to the historically correct paint color on the wide-board wooden siding.

Jon stepped out of the car, grabbed his bag from the back, and took his time making his way up the stone walkway to the side door facing the driveway. He knocked twice before letting himself in. Any resemblance between his parents' house and the Lewis home ended at the doorway. While the kitchen here had period-perfect wide board flooring and cabinets, it also had every cutting-edge kitchen aid, despite the minimal time either of his parents spent cooking. It also had a sterile quality that contrasted sharply with the homey country kitchen atmosphere of Kate's family home.

"Jon, is that you?" his mother called from the equally perfectly appointed dining room adjacent to the kitchen. "I was on my way to answer the door." She appeared in the doorway frowning.

"Hello, Mother." He took the frown to mean he should have waited outside until she got to the door. "How's Father."

She threw up her hands. "He's only been home two hours and he's irritable and impatient to be doing things he's not supposed to be doing yet. If he were his own patient, he'd be referring himself to another surgeon."

"Where should I put my bag?"

"Lynda has the guest room next to your father's room made up for you."

The room that had been his before he'd moved out. Jon smiled to himself at the mention of the housekeeper his parents had had since he was in high school. No doubt they paid her well, but he'd often thought her a saint for what she put up with, working for his parents.

"Is Lynda here? I'd like to say hello?"

"No, I gave her the afternoon off, so she can come in tomorrow afternoon and evening to help you. Your father as a patient is two-person job."

"Okay. I'll take my stuff upstairs and check on Father."

"He's resting in the downstairs guest room, but wants to get up already."

"I'll help him."

His mother stepped back in the dining room to let him past her. "Then, if you're hungry, Lynda left you sandwiches in the refrigerator."

"Thanks. I already had something."

"Well, I suppose they'll keep until tomorrow."

Jon lifted his bag higher as if to make it a barrier between him and his mother's disapproval. "I'll, uh, be right back down."

"Good. Your father and I want to talk with you."

That was almost an incentive to take his time.

"Father," Jon said as he entered the downstairs bedroom after dropping his bag in his old room.

His father nodded. "So you came. I told your mother I didn't need a babysitter."

Jon stepped toward the bed. "How are you feeling?"

"Fine, except for being tired of resting." His father sat up, feet dangling over the side of the bed. "Give me a hand."

His father leaned on Jon's arm as he slid off the bed to the floor slipped his feet into his slippers. Then, he let go of Jon's arm and began a shuffle to the doorway. "The dining room," he directed. "Your mother and I want to talk to you."

Jon followed, fully aware of what they wanted to talk about. *Grandpa.*

His mother was already sitting at the dining room table with papers in front of her when Jon and his father walked in and sat down.

"I had a real estate broker in Hudson give me an esti-mate of what she could sell the house and land for," his mother began, sliding a paper to Jon. "A lot of people from the city are buying old farms in Columbia County as second homes.

He glanced over the paper. The number looked about right to him, except it didn't account for the home equity loan Grandpa had taken.

"And," she continued, "the Firemen's Home in Hudson expects to have openings soon. The proceeds from the farm sale should cover the costs nicely for quite a while."

Jon stared numbly at the Firemen's Association of New York brochure about the organization's Firemen's Home for former volunteer firefighters. "Grandpa doesn't belong in a nursing home. He can take care of himself." *Mostly.* "If he couldn't, how could I be here helping with Father?" No need to mention the network he had for checking in on Grandpa.

"I made an appointment for you and your grandfather to tour the home next Wednesday," his mother said, as if Jon hadn't said anything.

Jon turned to his father for possible support.

His father was nodding in agreement. "He's your mother's father. She knows best."

Jon opened his mouth to say she didn't know anything about Grandpa. Then he looked, really looked at his father. At the moment, his father looked older than his grandfather. Sadness gripped Jon. He wasn't sure if it was for his father, his parents, himself, or the family they could have been.

Anger wiped out the sadness. "No."

"No, what?" his mother asked. "Should I reschedule?"

"No, I can't ... won't do it. First, I'm working at a mutual fund company in New York for the summer and can't take more time off."

"That's good. You wouldn't get anywhere financially, teaching at a community college. And all the more reason to get your grandfather settled somewhere else when you relocate in New York."

Jon gritted his teeth. "I don't plan on moving, and I'll still be teaching. More importantly, Grandpa doesn't need to be in a nursing home, and I refuse to have anything to do with putting him in one. Not to mention that he probably wouldn't qualify for a placement since his physical condition doesn't warrant full-time care."

His mother's expression hardened. "We can take care of him getting a proper assessment for placement. If we can't, I'll research some senior living facilities with independent and assisted living options."

Jon gave up trying talk sense with his mother. "If you plan on hounding me all weekend, I'll go to a hotel."

His mother jerked a wave-off to him. "Do as you please. I have Lynda coming to stay with your father tomorrow when I'll be at the gala."

Jon's father *harrumphed* as his contribution to the conversation.

"I'm going out." Jon tossed off the weight on his chest that accompanied his words.

It shouldn't matter, wasn't any worse than he might have expected. But they were his parents. Maybe he hadn't done a stupid thing, accepting Kate's sister and mother's invitation to the party tomorrow. It beat sitting alone in a hotel room.

He glanced from his mother to his father. Or here alone with his parents.

~

"HEY, SLEEPYHEAD." Ava burst into Kate's room. "Since you ditched me for lunch, I'm taking you to dinner."

Kate sat up. "I'm so sorry. I forgot about our lunch date." She stretched. She hadn't really been asleep. More thinking with her eyes closed. Too often about Jon. "Sure. Give me a minute to change and comb my hair."

"I wasn't thinking any place fancy," Ava said, not making any movement to leave.

"At least let me change my shirt." Kate stood and pointed toward the door. "Shoo, I'll be right down."

Kate changed into a fancier T with cut-out shoulders, let her hair down and brushed it, and touched up her make-up. She kicked off her athletic shoes and replaced them with leather sandals. After all, they might run into someone she knew. A picture of Jon appeared in her mind. She shook her head. Hadn't she seen enough of him at work and on the drive here?

She wiggled her freed toes and joined Ava in the living room.

"I thought we'd go to London's," Ava said, heading toward the front door.

"Sounds good to me." Kate restrained her surprise.

London's was a locally owned, mid-range family restaurant and bar.

"Why the surprise?" Ava asked.

So much for hiding her feelings.

"You didn't think I was going to say McDonald's, did you?"

Kate's gaze dropped to her feet as she pulled open the passenger door of Ava's car. "It *was* your favorite place."

"When I was a kid."

Kate swallowed. That's how she thought of Ava. As a kid. She studied her sister's profile, so much like Kate's own and their mother's. Where had the time gone? Ava wasn't a kid anymore. She was a woman who'd finished her education and achieved the first step in her career goals.

"What? Do I have dirt on my face or something?" Ava asked, digging in her bag beside her. She pulled out a jeweler's box.

"No squirt. Just realizing you're all grown up. Done with college, a teacher ..." Kate's gaze fixed on her sister slipping her engagement ring on her finger. "A woman engaged to be married."

Ava reached across the seat to show Kate a tasteful platinum solitaire diamond ring. "The matching wedding band is plain, but Trey's has a small diamond."

"It's beautiful." Kate smiled to cover any reaction to the pang in her heart. "You'll make a beautiful bride."

"Thank you," Ava said, placing her left hand on the steering wheel and turning the car on.

Kate relaxed against the seat back. She must have done a better job of masking her feelings this time. A founding member of the No Brides Club did not get wistful over engagement rings.

"How about you?"

"What?" Had she missed something Ava had said?

Ava turned onto the road toward town. "You and your to-die-for hunk of a chauffeur/employee."

Kate's heart skipped. "Jon? What about Jon?"

Ava grinned. "It must be fun being able to officially boss your boyfriend around at work."

"What *are* you talking about?"

"I saw the way you two looked at each other."

Kate leaned her elbow on the armrest of the door and rubbed her forehead. "And how was it we looked at each other?"

"Like there was more in play than hitching a ride home."

"Sorry to burst your romance bubble, but I had no idea where Jon was or what he was doing until my boss introduced him as my new assistant on Monday. Even then, I almost didn't recognize him." If she emphasized the *almost*, that was the truth. "He's changed a lot since high school."

Ava's eyes went soft and dreamy, and Kate bit back an admonishment to watch the road.

"But didn't you two date or something in high school?" her sister pressed. "Like what Jon said when you introduced us."

"Mathletes. We were on the Genesee High School team. Jon's parents are doctors and often couldn't drive him to regular competitions. So he rode with us."

Thinking about it now, Kate didn't know how they could have been busier than her dairy-farmer father. Not that it mattered.

"We hung out in different groups. Mathletes was about his only extracurricular activity. I was in student government, on the yearbook committee, prom committee, intramural sports, other stuff. Not to be mean"—although she had been in high school—"but he was a chunky nerd back then."

"Seriously?" Ava asked.

"Seriously." Who knew the beautiful swan that would emerge when Jon grew into his features and lost weight.

Ava flicked the turn signal to turn into the restaurant. "Wow! I can't begin to imagine him as nerdy-looking."

"You can look at my yearbooks when we get home."

Ava brought the car to a stop in the parking lot. "You admit that he's gorgeous now, right?"

"Yes, he's gorgeous." It wasn't hard to agree with the truth. "And he's always been intelligent and interesting." The note of wistfulness in her voice surprised Kate.

"So why don't you go for it?"

Kate sighed. "Because I'm concentrating on my career."

"You're not still in that No Brides Club thing?" Ava turned the car off and looked at her.

"Yes, my colleagues and I still meet Thursday nights." Kate knew she sounded pompous, but Ava was starting to get on her nerves. "Our careers are our top priority."

Her sister's eyes clouded. "Are you saying I'm not serious about my work?"

Kate touched her sister's hand. "Not at all. Some people just aren't cut out for serious relationships."

"And you think you're one of those people."

Kate nodded. "Besides, Jon will only be in the city for the summer. In the fall, he'll be back home teaching at Columbia-Greene Community College in Hudson and running his beef cattle operation."

Ava's eyes brightened, and Kate's stomach sank. Why had she said that, as if she would be interested in him if he was staying in the city?

~

JON HAD SECOND, third, and fourth thoughts as he walked from the side field off the driveway to the Lewis's back yard for Ava's graduation party. He hadn't gotten a hotel room yesterday. But the strain of breakfast with his parents this morning with his mother making another pitch for selling Grandpa's farm out from under him had been too much. This time she'd held out a bribe of replacing his sold BMW, ostensibly to celebrate his new job with DeBakker-Geld. Somehow his parents had wiped his teaching in the fall from their memories.

He had never been so glad to see anyone as he was when Lynda arrived shortly after noon and assured him she'd be fine with his father while Jon went to the party. He rounded the corner of the Lewis's house and slowed his pace when he spotted Kate in a bright blue and green sundress. The slight breeze molded the light fabric to her legs. His mouth went dry.

She gestured with her hand and laughed, making some point to the guy she was talking to. A guy about their age that he didn't recognize.

He hadn't considered that Kate might be involved with someone back here. After all, her sister had thought he and Kate were together when he'd dropped Kate off. She hadn't said anything about being in a relationship. Jon stopped and raked his hand through his hair. Why would she? Kate was his boss. He wasn't in the habit of discussing his boss's or any colleague's love life. His mind choked at the word *love*. What was with him? His interest in Kate had been over long ago, a silly high school crush he'd left in high school. Jon rubbed the back of his neck. Being in Western New York, in Genesee, was getting to him more than usual.

He glanced around. No one had noticed him. He could go back and help Lynda with his father. He turned to leave.

"Jon," a female voice called.

It sounded like Kate, but not exactly like Kate. He pivoted back around. Ava waved to him from the back step. She must have just come out of the house. *Too late to make a get-away*. Besides, despite the weirdness he was experiencing, the graduation party looked to be a better time than he'd have at his parents' house. And what else did he have to do?

"You made it," Ava said. "We're about to cut the cake, but you can get a burger or hot dog and stuff first if you want." She motioned with her left hand toward a grill on the patio and the sun glinted off her ring, catching his eye.

Ava followed his gaze and, blushing, covered her left hand with her right. "We haven't told my parents yet."

"I won't say anything. And I already had lunch, so I'll wait for the cake." He scanned the small crowd for anyone he knew besides Kate.

Ava grabbed his arm. "Kate's over there, if that's who you're looking for." Ava's smile was far too wide and knowing for someone her age.

"I was checking to see if I knew anyone else here," he said, as she tugged him toward Kate and the guy.

"Do you?"

He shook his head.

"They're mostly my friends, neighbors, and relatives. Kate hasn't stayed close with any of her high school friends."

Thinking back to high school, that was a plus in his book, not that Kate had been kinder than anyone else in her group. He'd idolized the teenage Kate, but genuinely liked the adult version—at least, as much as he'd seen.

"Look who I found," Ava called to Kate and the guy, who was smiling and nodding at whatever Kate had said to him.

Jon fisted and unfisted his hand. Why hadn't he gone when he'd had the chance? Or, better yet, never come to the party or Genesee.

"Jon," Kate said, her eyes widening. "Is there something wrong at home, with your grandfather? I left my cell phone in the house if you tried reach me."

Jon shook his head. No smiles for him. He wanted to spit in disgust at himself.

"No, I invited him to the party yesterday. Didn't I tell you?" Ava asked. The glint in her eyes belied her innocent expression.

Kate wrinkled her forehead, making his presence seem unwanted. He could have stayed at his parents' if that was the case.

"Pastor Chris, this is Kate's *friend* Jon Smith," Ava introduced him.

The guy was a minister. A rush of relief flowed through Jon. *But that didn't mean anything. He was still a guy.* Jon pasted a smile on his face and shook the man's hand. "Nice to meet you."

"The same," the guy said, not looking very minister-like in jean shorts and a polo shirt stretched across his chest.

"Chris and his wife are the new ministers at my parents' church," Kate said.

Knowing that her words had to be for his benefit, Jon wondered if he was as transparent with his out-of-control and unfounded jealousy. Ridiculous as it was, he couldn't call the feeling anything but jealousy. He corralled the remnants of his teenage self and shut them away.

Ava continued, "Kate and Jon went to high school together and now they work together in New York."

Kate rolled her eyes and Jon stifled a snort. Could Ava be any more obvious?

"You guys don't mind if I borrow Pastor Chris, do you? Trey and I are going to make our announcement now."

Kate glanced from her sister to Jon.

"Jon saw my ring." Ava responded to Kate's raised eyebrow.

"Are you sure you don't want to tell Mom and Dad in private first?" Kate asked.

"You're still behind me with Mom and Dad, aren't you?" Ava asked.

Jon couldn't help but pick up the sudden tension between Kate and Ava.

"Come on, Pastor Chris. Let's go find Trey and your wife." Ava took a step away from their circle and looked over her should at Kate. "Just because you and your No Brides Club friends don't believe in marriage doesn't mean it's a bad thing."

"Excuse me," the minister said, I'd better go with her.

"I ... she ... I have to go, too." Kate took off after Ava and Chris, leaving Jon standing alone in the middle of the yard, stuck on Ava's words.

No Brides Club? What was that? And why should it bother him that Kate belonged?

CHAPTER 5

*S*orry about yesterday. Ready to leave anytime you are.

Kate took a break from cleaning up after breakfast and texted Jon. Her parents and Ava had left for church. Kate had begged off, saying Jon wanted to get an early start. She stared out the kitchen window, her gaze going to the middle of the yard where she'd left Jon yesterday to go mend fences with Ava.

Ava and Trey's big announcement had gone off without a hitch. Kate wasn't sure what had made her apprehensive about supporting her sister at the last moment. It turned out that their parents weren't surprised in the least and were happy for the young couple. After that, talk had turned to congratulations and wedding stories, and Kate had gone in search of Jon but he'd left.

She pulled her gaze from the window and checked her phone, even though she hadn't heard a ding signaling a reply from Jon. It wasn't that, as Ava had accused, she didn't believe in marriage. Ava and Trey's obvious joy in each other, catching her mother and father last night in a close embrace in the living room when they hadn't heard her enter, the adorable Edna and Ralph at the train station, they all warmed her heart. *It's just that I have other things to accomplish first. More important things. For now, at least.*

Her phone dinged and set her heart racing. *Jon.* She rolled her shoulders as if they would shake off whatever was afflicting her.

She read the text. Nothing to apologize for. I'll be there in a half hour.

I'll be ready, she typed. Kate glanced around the kitchen. Nothing left to do in here. Her bag was packed. She could check her work email, although she'd done that yesterday morning to catch up on anything that had happened on Friday. Kate trudged upstairs and got her overnight bag and tablet.

She dropped her bag next to the couch and herself onto the couch and powered up her tablet, drumming her fingers on the armrest while she waited for the login box to appear. At the prompt she typed her password and skimmed her new mail. The last email, from Bob, dated Saturday afternoon, grabbed her attention.

Subject: Monday Strategy Meeting

Note the new time: 9:30

But it wasn't the content that had her fixed on the email. It was the required attendees. The list included jpsmith. *Jon.* There weren't any J-anything Smiths at her senior analyst level or above. Since when had lower level staff been included? She narrowed her eyes and scanned the attendees again. It wasn't all the lower level analysts. It was only Jon. Good thing she'd decided to forego the day off she'd scheduled for tomorrow to decompress from the trip to Genesee.

It took all Kate's strength not to heave the tablet across the room. The uncertainty about why Jon had been included in the meeting rubbed against the argument she'd had with herself about marriage and career—and first things first. She couldn't let her guard down, or Jon just might get *her* promotion. Somehow, reasserting her resolve didn't give her the boost it usually did.

The sound of a car pulling into the driveway brought her to her feet. Kate stashed her tablet in her shoulder bag and looked out the window. *Jon. Early.* She put her bag on her shoulder and picked up her case. She was ready.

"Hey." Jon walked around his car to open the passenger side door.

"Hi." She closed the door behind her and met him at the car.

"I'm early, but I see you're ready."

She slid into the passenger side. "Yes, yes, I am."

He cocked his head and closed the door without saying anything.

"How's your dad?" Getting Jon to talk about his family and other small-talk topics had worked to fill the silence on the drive here.

"He's all right."

"Your mother will be okay with him until tomorrow?" She tried to pull out his terse statement.

"Fine. She asked Lynda, their housekeeper, to come in yesterday and this afternoon."

"That's how you got to come to Ava's party."

"Something like that." Jon flicked the directions and flexed his left hand before placing it back on the steering wheel. "Sorry, my parents spent our breakfast time together trying to convince me that Grandpa should be in a nursing home or at least some kind of senior living facility, and I should sell the farm to pay for it."

"Oh." That explained his mood. "As you texted me, no

apologies needed. I know how it is. The culture shock of coming from the city to Genesee to visit family." She slapped her fingertips to her lips. Jon lived with family, his grandfather. In the country.

"For me it's the company, not the culture."

With the meeting email and her new-found resolve foremost in her mind, Kate shouldn't have cared about his parents or anything else that would move their relationship off the colleagues/coworkers plain. But she felt for Jon being an only child. She'd had her sister and brother as potential allies in disagreements with her parents. "Should I put on some music?" she reached for the audio knob.

"Sure."

"What we listened to on the way?"

"Fine."

After ten miles of silently taking in the scenery of the Montezuma National Wildlife Refuge out her window, a site she'd seen countless times before, the sound of the radio wasn't enough.

"Did you check your work email this morning?" Kate asked to initiate a conversation not about family or their personal lives. Keep it professional, or at least neutral.

"Pardon? My mind was elsewhere."

"Your work email. You should have gotten a message from Bob about a meeting, sent yesterday.

Jon made a sound that could have been a laugh or a snort. "I'm going to admit to not even bringing my tablet with me *to* check my work email. Bad employee?"

"I wouldn't say that." But it didn't sound like someone who was angling for a permanent position at the fund family. Her promotion. She studied his profile. The straight nose, strong jawline. Studied it too long.

He turned toward her with s smile. "Do I have raspberry jam or maybe egg on my face."

"No." She fumbled. I was ..." She couldn't tell him she was trying to read whether he was feigning disinterest in work or truthfully wanted a position at DeBakker only for the summer. The old, high-school Jon wouldn't have been smooth enough to fool her. Or maybe she'd underestimated him then—and was now.

She cleared her throat. "We meet the Strategy Group the first Monday of the month. As my assistant, you were added to the attendees." By whom, she wasn't sure. Bob or those higher ups he'd referred to.

"Sounds like it could be interesting."

Kate went on to explain a typical meeting, with Jon making comparisons to the way things were handled at the hedge fund he'd worked at in Boston. When they wore that topic out, Kate rested her head against the seat headrest, closed her eyes and enjoyed the warm summer sun on her face. And, true to form, she felt herself drift off to sleep.

She didn't wake up until Jon was slowing down the car for the Thruway exit at Catskill, to drop Kate off at the Hudson train station.

"You're with me again."

"Yes, I do have a habit of sleeping on trips if I'm not driving." And it had stopped them from veering off into any personal conversation.

"I was thinking," he said pulling away from the tollbooth. "you should come up to our place some weekend. Get out of the city. Meet my grandpa. He said he remembers me talking about you when I was a kid."

Kate didn't know where that invitation had come from, nor what underlying meaning it might have. But if she was surprised by his invitation, it wasn't half as much as she was by her almost immediate reply.

"I think I'd like that."

Jon wasn't sure why he'd invited Kate to spend a weekend at the farm, but he did know he had to stop dwelling on it. The extra time added to his commute while a crew cleared debris from the track wasn't helping. He'd already finished the book he'd brought for the ride and checked his email twice, alerting Kate to his delay and accepting Bob's meeting invitation, although now he might not make it to the office by 9:30. He'd missed the 6:40 train out of Rhinebeck and had had to wait for the 7 o'clock one. Even if he took a cab instead of the subway as usual, there'd be the extra time spent fighting other financial district commuters for a ride.

The conductor stepped into the business section car. "Folks, the debris has been cleared. We'll be moving momentarily, expecting to arrive at Penn Station about 20 minutes off schedule."

Jon tapped his email app to let Kate know his ETA. He should be able to just make the meeting. Granted the job was only temporary, but he was barely into his second week with DeBakker, and this was his first corporate meeting. It wouldn't be good to miss it, especially since he was the only junior analyst he recognized on the meeting list. He assumed Kate had asked that he attend, to bring him up to speed on the work he'd be doing.

When he'd reached Penn Station, Jon had lucked out with a rideshare to the office. He hit his cubicle at 9:15, dropped his stuff and stepped across the aisle to Kate's. "Hey."

Kate spun her chair to face him. "Jon, you did make it."

"Yep. Anything I need to know before we go?"

"Not, really. I'll be ready in a minute." She turned back to her laptop.

Jon retreated to his cubicle and chugged the coffee he'd grabbed on his way to his desk. Somehow he'd expected something more, something different from Kate this morning. He placed his cup on the desk. What? An atta-boy for making the meeting? He had to admit that dashing off the train and catching the rideshare to arrive at the office with plenty of time to make the meeting had revived some of the old adrenalin of his busy Boston days. And while the feeling had been good, he knew that another investment services position wasn't what he wanted long-term.

"Ready?" Kate stood at his cubicle entrance.

"Okay, if I bring my coffee?"

"Sure."

They headed for the conference room, Jon expecting some direction from Kate, despite her answer to his earlier question. His weekend in Genesee had affected him in more ways than solidifying his determination to help Grandpa maintain his independence. He'd spent the last part of the train ride and the car ride envisioning the meeting. What he'd pictured was Kate and him with their heads together, mapping out a united front, as they had when they'd worked together on the Mathletes team. Why, he didn't know. He glanced sideways at Kate, who matched her stride to his, jaw set.

She knew something about the meeting he didn't and didn't want to share that information. "Is it usual to invite all new investment hires to one strategy meeting as an introduction to company processes?"

Kate's pace slowed nearly imperceptibly and then picked back up.

"I noticed Bob's meeting email didn't include anyone at my level that I've met."

"No."

Jon pursed his lips. What was with the monosyllable answers? "No, it isn't usual or no Bob didn't invite anyone else at my level."

"Both." Kate hesitated. "He made you part of the meeting because of your experience at the Boston hedge fund. He—"

"Kate." A man stepped out of the office they were passing.

She nodded. "Gregg."

"You must be our new guy, Jon Smith," Gregg cut her off before Kate could introduce him, if that had been her plan. She was acting so weird, almost as if she'd prefer he weren't around. Her way of keeping their professional contact separate from their personal relationship. Friendship. Whatever it was that had prompted him to invite her to the farm for a weekend and her to agree.

Gregg stepped in stride with them. "Gregg Hanley, Aggressive Growth Fund manager. I was on vacation last week. Good to have you on board. Your hedge fund was at the top of the rankings the last three years you managed it. Nice work."

Kate stiffened beside Jon, making him wonder if there was a rivalry or some other animosity between her and Gregg.

Jon tightened his shoulder blades. "Thanks. I'm hoping to get some different perspectives from the analysts' view while I'm here. For classes I'm teaching in the fall."

"Adjunct? I've done that a couple times. Not enough money for the time."

"No," Jon corrected. "I'm a full-time instructor at Columbia-Green Community College."

Confusion spread across Gregg's face. "I thought—"

"Jon. Kate," Bob interrupted Gregg as they stepped into the conference room. "Take the seats beside me, so I can introduce Jon."

Kate's jaw tightened as Bob motioned them to three empty chairs at the far end of the nearly full table. Jon stepped back to let Kate go first, and her stony expression softened. *This. The constant ebb and flow of undercurrents*, Jon thought, *was one of the reasons I left the hedge fund*. Foolishly, he'd thought he could avoid it here with his lower level position.

Bob waited for Kate, Gregg, and him to take their seats. "Before we start our reports, I want to introduce Jon Smith, a new analyst. As you all know, Jon comes to us well recommended from Boston's top hedge fund."

Jon resisted squirming in his seat as all eyes in the room turned toward him. Everyone knew? How? And why was his background so important? He'd made it clear when he'd interviewed for the assistant analyst position that he was here for that and that only, and only for the summer.

Bob continued, "Introduce yourself and your position with DeBakker before your report."

The reporting went around the table, starting with the fund managers, whose welcomes seemed to be a subtle form of lure-with-praise and dissect. They were followed by the senior analysts whose welcomes as a group weren't nearly as welcoming.

As the reporting came around to Kate last, Jon relaxed

with the thought that the meeting was almost over. Or at least his part in it was.

As Kate opened her report folder, a man Jon hadn't met yet entered the conference room.

"David DeBakker," she whispered.

One of the senior partners.

She cleared her throat to begin her report.

"Kate, let Smith, handle the report," Mr. DeBakker said. "Give his view. So we can see his mettle."

Her mouth snapped shut, and she pushed the folder to Jon. Her hurt, perhaps apparent only to him, wove itself around his chest and tightened.

He glanced at the pages. Kate had a short intro, followed by concise data and economic commentary in bullet points. Just as he would if he'd done the report. He could successfully wing this. Jon glanced at Kate to give her a silent affirmative and immediately returned his gaze to the report. If the virtual spikes of tension radiating from her had been actual spikes, he'd be a dead man, as would most of the rest of the meeting attendees. Maybe he should reevaluate the "good luck" of his catching the rideshare this morning after the train delay.

UNBELIEVABLE. Kate had half a mind to tender her resignation then and there. The other half, the rational unemotional one, said she wasn't giving up her promotion that easily. The opening for the Growth and Income Fund Manager position had to be what this nonsense was all about. She tapped her fingers on the table as Jon started the report, reading her introductory words. She relaxed slightly against the back of the chair as he continued, using her bullet-point observations without any commentary from him, as she'd expect an assistant to do.

"Thanks, Smith. That was Kate's report. What's *your* outlook for the quarter for growth and income?"

Kate clenched her jaw. She shouldn't let it get to her, but Mr. DeBakker addressing Jon as Smith and her as Kate did.

"I've only been here four days, and most of my prior experience is in venture capital and addressing the strategic resource needs of lower middle-market companies, not general growth and income investing."

That didn't sound like a guy who was hot for her job, current or future.

"But ..."

Kate straightened in her seat. *Here it comes.*

"My assessment is the same."

A frown flashed on DeBakker's face as he glanced from Jon to Bob. "You did receive the email about our opening for an investment manager for the Growth and Income Fund?" he asked as if to qualify his expectations of Jon.

"Yes, sir, I did." Jon crossed his arms over his chest.

DeBakker nodded, and a rustle went around the table. He must be the *from above* Bob had referred to in answer to her question about Jon receiving the open position bulletin from HR.

"I'm going to be frank," DeBakker said. "We'd like you to join DeBakker permanently."

Gazes from the other senior analysts—some gloating and some pitying, depending on whether they were competing for the promotion—and the fund managers focused en masse on Kate. She briefly wished a sink hole would open in the floor and suck her in.

No! Her spine stiffened. She wasn't going to lay down and

roll over. She needed this promotion if she wanted to buy her apartment and escape the toxic culture to any decent position with another firm. She'd been a senior analyst here longer than the industry average for fund managers, which would be a minus if she applied elsewhere if she didn't get the promotion.

"... be frank." Jon's voice pulled her back into the meeting.

"As I told Bob and HR, I don't see my tenure here as anything more than a summer learning experience for the college courses I'll be teaching full time in the fall."

"I admire your honesty," DeBakker said. "But don't write us off too quickly. DeBakker-Glem can use a *man* with your background."

Had DeBakker really emphasized *man*? Or was she over-sensitive? Winces from a few of the others, female and male said he had.

"I appreciate your confidence in me, but I assure you my short time here has shown me that I have a long way to go to match Kate's and probably others' acumen in the growth and income sector."

Kate willed herself not to blush, uncertain whether the warmth flowing through her was from Jon's praise in front of everyone or because the praise had come from Jon. And she couldn't help but take some solace in the fact that DeBakker looked as uncomfortable as she felt. People didn't often turn down an offer from DeBakker-Glem, especially one from a senior partner made as publicly as the offer made to Jon. The warmth left as quickly as it had come. Jon's equally public shutdown might reflect badly on her, as his supervisor.

DeBakker left the conference room with a "I'll let you get on with your meeting."

"All right," Bob said. "Kate, do you have anything to add?"

Her mind blanked. In reference to what?

"To your and Jon's report and quarterly recommendations?" Bob prompted.

Her uncharacteristic loss of control over herself and her internal thoughts was not the way to work herself into the almost all-male domain of fund management. She got a grip on her professional self. "Yes. One small point, a tweak to my Treasury Bill weighting recommendation based on Kim's"— the only female portfolio manager currently at DeBakker—"income fund group's report."

"Email us your updated report." Bob said.

"I'll have it to you early afternoon."

"Great. Anyone have anything else?" Bob looked around the table. "Then, let's get to work."

The managers and analysts began shuffling out. Kate held back to catch her fellow senior analyst on Kim's team and ask him to forward her the source for the new data he'd used for his report. She hadn't had time this morning to go over everything that had come in Friday and update her projected outlook for the meeting.

That's what I get for taking time off from this place. Kate gathered her report folder from the table on her way out. But it had been good to see her family and kick back in a slower paced environment for a couple of days.

"Eek!" Kate slapped her free palm against her chest as she exited the conference room. Jon stood right outside, leaning a shoulder against the wall. Her surprise was replaced by admiration for how cool and calm Jon had been in the back and forth with Mr. DeBakker—in contrast to her tightly strung and double knotted nerves. And she'd only been peripherally involved.

"I didn't mean to startle you. Fred waylaid me for a few words. Then, I saw you were on your way out, so I waited."

Fred. The Growth and Income Fund manager who was retiring.

Jon pushed away from the wall. Somewhere between yesterday and today, she'd forgotten how tall he was. Not that his height had anything to do with the business at hand.

"Fred had questions about the report. Positive questions."

Kate swallowed. Was her internal upheaval that apparent that Jon had to add that the questions had been positive? If so, David DeBakker's appearance at the meeting had thrown her even more off kilter than she'd thought.

"I told him I hadn't worked on it, so he'd need to check with you."

"Thanks, I'll touch base with him when I send the revised report."

As they approached their work area, Jon looked around over his right, then left shoulder. He dropped his voice. "David DeBakker. Does he drop in on your strategy meetings often?"

"Like he did today? Never. You're quite the draw."

Jon laughed. "Yeah, I think at least half the people in the room mentally drew a bull's eye on me."

"That would be about right. All the senior analysts."

"Including you?" He didn't wait for an answer. "There's nothing wrong with the Growth and Income Fund Manager position, is there?"

"No," she answered to both of his questions.

"Seems like the manager position should be yours. If you want it."

It wasn't easy to resist accepting Jon's compliment at face

value. She wanted to, wanted to know he respected her as a professional equal. But there was that one niggling doubt in her that said he could be setting her up for a fall.

"Grab your laptop and let's go work on my report revisions in the small conference room." *Where no one can overhear us.*

He raised an eyebrow at her non-response.

A minute later, Kate shut the door to the small conference room behind her and Jon. He took a seat and opened his laptop. She started for the seat next to him, but decided on the one across the table instead. *Arm's length*, she reminded herself. Kate rested her hands on her closed laptop and looked across the table at him. *The man was model handsome.* Kate bit her tongue. First, his height. Now … What was her brain doing, letting emotional observations break through like that? *This was business*, and she routinely worked with several attractive single men without any of this nonsense clouding her thoughts.

"Yes, to answer your question, I want the portfolio manager position, as I wanted the last fund manager opening and the one before it."

"But the Growth and Income Fund is your fund. I would think it would be a given to promote you."

Yeah, I would, too, but I know better. "The atmosphere in the meeting was an accurate cross-section of the culture here."

Another raised eyebrow fixed her gaze on his eyes. She hadn't noticed before, but his eyes weren't actually blue. They were more aquamarine. Kate dropped a hand to her lap and pinched herself. *We're business associates.* And she'd made a policy of keeping everyone she worked with at an arm's length. Her gaze dropped to his arms. The thin cloth of his crisp dress shirt did little to hide the outline of the muscles that lay beneath—muscles that the t-shirts he'd worn on the drive to and from Genesee had given her an up-close view of.

Kate cleared her throat. "My plan is to get the position this round and work it a couple years for a step up to something bigger at another firm with more opportunity for women."

Jon studied her with an intense expression she remembered from school, the expression he'd get when he was trying to crack a difficult math problem.

She snapped her mouth shut. That wasn't exactly what she'd planned to say. Nor did she particularly want him analyzing her words. That was more like something she'd share with the No Brides members. She was out of control. The companionable drive to and from Genesee had lulled her into putting Jon into the friend category. She needed to shove him back into her coworker one.

"You can cross my former employer off your list, if you're wondering," he said, losing the pensive look.

"It's not on the list. I'd rather stay in New York. I do have a work question, though."

"Shoot."

"What's your interest in the portfolio manager position?"

CHAPTER 6

On Thursday, Kate stepped out onto the sidewalk, the heavy humid air a welcome relief from the precisely cooled air inside her office building. She'd never gotten Jon's answer to her question. Before he could speak, Bob had breezed into the room and whisked Jon away on some special project that had kept him working on the far side of the cubicle maze for the past three and a half days. In exchange, she'd been lent a new female junior analyst. The young woman was more cutthroat than many of the men Kate worked with. And unlike with Jon, Kate knew what the woman's answer to her question would be.

By the time she reached the Briarwood Tavern rooftop, her damp suit had her wishing she'd taken a cab or at least hadn't made the short trip a powerwalk. Kate made her way to the bar.

"The usual," she said to the bartender Andre.

"The usual usual or the new usual?" Andre grinned.

"I'll stick with the usual usual." Her day had been trying, but nothing extremely out-of-the-ordinary had happened to make her go monster-size this week. *Hey,* the Stable Growth

Fund Manager had even emailed her to get her take on some new speculations his senior analyst had come up with. Almost like an equal.

"Here you go, one regular fresh cherry margarita."

"Thanks, Andre" Kate surveyed the room for her friends and checked the clock behind the bar. Only a little after five. She must be the first one here. She made her way to the back and staked claim on two four-seat tables. They could push them together if everyone showed. Lately, the group had fallen out of its habit of sending around a text the evening before to confirm their meeting, so she didn't know who to expect.

A short while later, Julie stopped by the table to let Kate know she was there. "I think we may be the only ones again tonight," Julie said. "It appears the male species has made a serious inroad in our No Brides bailiwick," she observed of the other members' recent domino-effect fall into love.

Kate peered at her half-gone margarita. "No chance of that happening with me. I'm putting all my energy into my promotion battle." *Except for the times my work doesn't take all my thought power and Jon fills the empty space.* She pushed the margarita a couple inches away. She'd better slow down or she'd run the risk of becoming downright maudlin.

Julie pulled her wallet from her bag and hung the bag on the seat across from Kate. "I'll grab a drink and be right back."

"I'll be here." Kate nursed her drink until Julie returned.

"Guess who I saw come in when I was leaving the bar?" Julie said, placing her drink on the table across from Kate.

Kate did a quick inventory of friends and acquaintances they had in common. She came up blank. "I give up."

Julie leaned toward Kate, and in a conspiratorial tone said, "Mr. Eye Candy from the other week."

Jon! "Where?"

"Look past me to the left."

Kate looked, then lifted her arm, and waved when his gaze connected with hers. So much for her confirming it was Jon without him seeing her,

"What are you doing?" Julie's voice rose with each word.

"Sit. We haven't talked recently," Kate said. She'd skipped last Thursday's meeting to get ready for her weekend trip to Genesee. A pang of guilt vibrated through her. At one time, she wouldn't have waited for their weekly meeting to share the news. She would have been right on the phone, texting all the group members about her new assistant. "I missed last week's meeting, and you were out of town."

Julie sat and tapped the table with her splayed fingertips. "Who is he?"

"Hey." Jon appeared at their table before Kate could answer.

"Hi. Did you miss your train?" So far as she could tell from last week and the office buzz, Jon had been out of the office and headed to Penn by five every afternoon since he'd started work, which Kate had put in her mental no-column tally as to whether he wanted a permanent position at DeBakker.

"No," Jon said.

"Don't look now." Julie interrupted, "but you just lost your table. By the way, I'm Julie Harrison."

"Sorry," Kate said, looking more at Jon than Julie.

"No need for apologies. I'm Jon Smith. Kate and I went to high school together."

Julie lifted her drink. "Ah, so you dated or something?"

Both Kate and Jon laughed.

"More like avoided each other like the plague, which

isn't easy when your entire high school has only about 400 students," Kate said.

Julie's expression shouted, *Were you nuts?* Jon stilled, his face expressionless.

Kate's throat tightened. She'd offended him, fallen into age-old behavior. He hadn't really avoided her, although he should have, given how she and her friends treated him. And she hadn't actually avoided him either.

She pasted a smile on her face. "And Jon is my new summer assistant."

Julie leaned on her elbow closest to Jon and cupped her hand around the side of her mouth. "Lucky you," she mouthed.

"Yes." The word rose way above the din of the bar. "Jon has jumped into the position with both feet."

"I see." Julie eyed them both.

What did Julie see? That Jon could be more than simply her assistant/coworker if she let him. Which she didn't plan on doing. Not that Jon had given her any signal that he would want to be. Besides DeBakker-Glem frowned on boss-employee relationships.

"Join us," Julie said.

"Only to finish my Coke." He raised his half-full glass in a toast motion.

While Jon took a seat between them, Kate analyzed Julie's invitation and his stopping in the bar, paying bar prices for a Coke. The No Brides Club didn't have a set of rules, but it was universally understood that the group was women only. And she couldn't very well talk to Julie about Jon, the meeting Monday, or him being grabbed away from her for a special project the rest of the week with him sitting right here. Of course, it wasn't much of a group or meeting with just her and Julie.

Her gaze fixed on his drink. As for the Coke, maybe he was meeting someone here and wanted to be at his sharpest for the meeting. Someone from DeBakker? That fanned a doubt in her about Jon being interested only in his summer position that her mental rundown of what she couldn't talk about in front of him had started. She put that doubt in the yes-column of her mental tally.

"Julie are you in financial services, too?" Jon asked

"No, I'm a software developer. Kate and I were room-mates at NYU and stayed in touch after we both found jobs in the city."

The bar server from the other evening stopped by their table. "Jon, can I get you or you ladies anything else?"

"No we're good." Kate crossed her arms in front of her. "Thanks," she added, softening her too-sharp words and covertly studying Jon for any reaction to the server remembering his name. She didn't see any, but that could explain Jon being here. For all Kate knew, he stopped in every evening after work.

"Okay, let me know if you do," the server said.

Julie's gaze trailed after the server. She tilted her face toward Jon. "Do you come here often?"

"Nope, only my second time."

Kate gripped her drink. *And the server had remembered his name.* Not that Jon had seemed surprised.

"I didn't think so, at least not on Thursday nights."

Her friend's unspoken, *I would have noticed*, had Kate clenching the glass now, for no discernible reason. Why shouldn't Julie or any woman notice Jon? He was certifiably noticeable. She lifted the drink to her lips and took a gulp, nearly dropping the glass when she heard a cell phone ring close by over the bar noise.

"That's mine," Julie said, pulling the phone from her bag

and glancing at the screen. "I have to take it." Her cheeks reddened before she turned to stand and walk a short distance away.

"Interesting," Kate said aloud to herself.

"Pardon?" Jon said.

"Nothing." Kate waved her hand back and forth a couple of inches above the table. "You never said what kept you here this evening. Normally, you'd probably be halfway home by now."

"Yes, and looking forward to getting there." He rubbed his forehead.

"So?"

"Gregg called a 7 a.m. project meeting for tomorrow."

Kate strained not to clench her hands into fists. It wasn't her project. There was no reason she should have known about the meeting. Or care. But she did.

"I decided to stay over at The Greenwich."

"Then, you'll need dinner. We usually order something here," Kate said as Julie returned to the table.

"No, thanks. I'm going to grab my gym stuff from the hotel and go swim laps, since I won't make my usual workout tomorrow morning before work."

"Oh, Okay," Kate stuttered, her mind picturing Jon in a form-fitting swim jammer suit like many competitive swimmers wore. From Julie's half smile, she might be, too.

"Besides, I understand the No Brides Club is women only."

"Ava strikes again!" Kate said, shaking her head.

Jon grinned. "Yep." He stood, tucking his chair back under the table. "Nice meeting you," he said to Julie, who'd finished her call and rejoined them.

"The pleasure was mine," she said.

Kate refrained from glaring at Julie.

"See you tomorrow, Kate."

"Right." Unless Jon was still tied up with the secret project he was working on with Gregg.

Julie picked her bag up from the back of her chair. "I've got to go, too. Something, uh, something has come up."

Something or someone? Kate remembered Julie's blush when she looked at her phone.

"Sure. I understand."

After Julie left, Kate stared at her now empty margarita glass. Her heart began pounding. Jon wouldn't tell the guys about her group, would he? It was the sort of thing her group in high school might have done, mocked a girls' club. But Jon wasn't like that. Or he hadn't been like that. But what did she know about him now? He'd been very successful in a cutthroat business.

Kate cradled her head in her hands. She should have ordered the monster size.

JON TOWEL DRIED HIS HAIR. The swim had done him good. But it had used up the carbs from the Coke he'd had at the Briarwood and the protein from the energy bar he'd wolfed down on the walk to the Equinox Gym. He was starved. Kate had said her group usually ate at the Briarwood Thursday evenings. He could go back there. Jon ran a comb through his hair, rolled his swimsuit in his towel and stuffed it in his gym bag. Maybe they'd still be there.

He pushed open the locker room door. *No.* She'd be with her friends and wouldn't want him around. Kate hadn't looked any too happy when he'd walked over to her and Julie and Julie had announced that he'd lost the table where he'd been sitting. He'd get some takeout and go back to his hotel room.

Jon stepped into the hall and blinked twice. It *was* Kate in yoga pants and a tank top, with her hair pulled up in a waterfall of curls rather than scraped back in the bun or whatever it was she did with her hair for work. The perfect "O" her mouth formed before she pushed a stray curl off her forehead said she'd spotted him, too.

Kate push a stray curl off her forehead. "Jon. Hi. I didn't know you'd be swimming here."

"I figured I might as well take advantage of the corporate membership."

"Right. Me, too. Yoga." Her expression flickered from surprise to flustered.

"So, your meeting broke up early."

"Something like that." Flustered turned to guarded.

He hoped he hadn't caused the early end. Jon reverted to his old habit of second-guessing-himself, something he thought he'd killed a long time ago. No, why would his stopping by her table have ended the meeting? From what Ava had told him about Kate and her friends' group, his presence would have only gotten the conversation going after he left.

"I, um, need to change." Kate pointed at the women's locker room door.

"Yeah." Although he liked the yoga version of Kate better than the buttoned-up version at work, as he'd liked the casual version of her last weekend.

She lifted her hand to push open the door.

"Wait. Have you eaten yet?"

"No."

"Do you want to get something with me? The two of us. After you change." His half-stuttered invitation was right out of his awkward nerd years. Like his brain couldn't move him and Kate out of high school. Jon rubbed the back of his neck, braced for her *no thank you* excuse.

"Sorry, I already ordered a pizza and need to hurry if I'm going to get home before it gets there."

"Okay, maybe another time." He gripped his gym bag and took a step.

"Wait. You could come over and we could share the pizza."

Kate was inviting him to her apartment. "Sure."

"Great, now I really need to get changed." Kate disappeared into the locker room.

Jon watched the door close. He wasn't going to read anything into that invitation. *Nope.* She was probably just being polite. Nor was he going to let his brain loose on the idea that Kate was disrobing on the other side of the wall. He was an adult.

Jon nodded at a guy walking by that he thought he remembered vaguely from DeBakker and moved to a bench in the hall a short distance from the locker rooms. Sitting here wouldn't look as stalkerish as standing across from the door to the women's locker room. He checked his work email—not that he expected to find anything of interest— and kept an eye out for Kate. Deep inside, he couldn't let go of the micro possibility that she might slip out without him. The old Kate might have thought something like that was funny. But he hadn't seen any hint of that version of Kate since he'd started working with her.

"A problem?"

His head shot up. "No, why?"

"Your expression. You looked deep in thought."

"Everything is fine." He pushed up from the bench and

walked her to the door, holding it open for her to go out first. "Subway or taxi?"

She smiled at him over her shoulder, making him grab the door tighter so it didn't slip out of his now sweaty hand.

"Neither, I live right up the street." She grabbed his hand and pulled him up the sidewalk. "And I think that's the pizza guy." She pointed at a car weaving through traffic.

He wrapped his hand around Kate's, wishing he'd rubbed it against his pant leg before she'd grabbed it and adjusted his gait to match hers. Maybe he could read a little into her inviting him to her place.

The delivery person dashed up the walk of a building two doors down, rang the intercom bell and tapped his foot while he waited.

"Apartment 211?" She shouted, breaking into a full run.

Jon half stumbled on the uneven sidewalk and picked up his pace, rather than let go of her hand.

She stopped in front of the deliverer, who was headed back to his car. "Is that a pepperoni pizza for Lewis, apartment 211? I'm Lewis."

The delivery person took a sidestep away from her.

"She's Lewis," Jon verified, holding his hand out for the pizza box.

"Just let me run upstairs for your tip," Kate said, disentangling her hand from Jon's.

"I'll cover it." He had his wallet out before she could answer and handed the guy a twenty.

The guy handed over the pizza. Jon's stomach growled at the spicy aroma rising from the box into the humid night air.

"I'd better get you upstairs and feed you."

"Good evening, Ms. Lewis." The doorman opened the door.

"Thank you, Michael."

As soon as Kate's back was to them, the doorman gave Jon a thorough inspection. The warning look the older man gave Jon was something he'd expect a father to give a daughter's first date. The itch the guy's look caused in that unreachable spot between Jon's shoulder blades almost prompted him say, *We're only having pizza.*

"Thank you," he said instead before striding across the lobby to join Kate at the elevator.

The elevator tinged its way down and they stepped in, the doors closing behind them. Kate pushed two.

"You have a great location, here," Jon said.

"Yes, I can walk to work, stores and the gym, and the building is great, too. We have a laundry, rooftop patio, a doorman, and a resident super, as well as parking—not that I have a car—and pets—not that I have time for one. I'm thinking of taking an offer I have to buy my place."

Jon glanced down at Kate, who stood shoulder-to-shoulder—or more precisely, shoulder to bicep—with him. *Yeah, the building was great. Except the unusually cramped elevator.* He moved his foot slightly to the left and hit the wall. *Small and slow moving and lacking ventilation.* He sucked in a breath, but couldn't fill his lungs.

Kate lifted her face to him and parted her lips.

If he leaned down ...

"Are you okay?" She asked. "You looked flushed."

He jerked back. "Fine." *Just almost indulging in a teenage fantasy.* "Hungry, from my swim. "That's all." *And not necessarily for pizza.*

"WELL, THEN," Kate said as the elevator doors opened. "I'd

better get you inside and feed you." *And put some distance between us before my imagination gets away from me.*

Jon held the elevator door for her, an ordinary smile curving his lips. As if anything was ordinary about him. Had she really thought he was going to kiss her in the elevator?

"This way." She pointed down the hall. "I'm in 211."

"So, you said before you ran down the pizza deliverer," Jon said with a chuckle.

"I shouldn't have shouted it." Kate shrugged. "What is that saying, you can take the girl out of the country, but you can't take the country out of the girl? Although, I've given it a good shot."

"And I've given in and embraced the country."

Kate unlocked her apartment. Was Jon purposely pointing out their differences? She opened the door and quickly inventoried the condition of the room, her gaze halting at the overflowing basket of clean laundry. Nothing visible that she wouldn't want Jon to see on top of the basket. *Or anywhere,* she corrected herself, giving herself a mental slap for letting her thoughts go in that direction. She was feeling the loss of support she'd gotten from the No Brides Club when it had been more active.

"Okay if I come in?" Jon asked.

"Yes, of course." She stepped in further so Jon could walk through the doorway. "You can put the pizza on the bar and pull up a stool."

He took his time walking across the living room. "This is a really nice place." He set the pizza box on the bar. "One bedroom?"

"Yes. Do you want a beer? Ice water? I could make coffee." She was babbling. But sadly, she could barely remember the last time she'd had a guy up to her apartment. *Your choice,* her professional self reminded her.

"Beer sounds good." He opened the pizza box.

Kate grabbed two bottles from the refrigerator and placed them on the end of the bar before taking two plates from the cupboard. "A fork?" She turned around to see Jon sitting at the bar, a folded piece of pizza cradled in a napkin headed for his mouth.

"Scratch that."

He stopped. "Sorry. I should have waited for you. I've been hanging out with guys too long."

"No need to apologize. If you went directly from the Briarwood to the Equinox, you must have been swimming well over an hour. You've got to be starving."

"I could have waited a minute for you. Sit, please."

Kate placed a plate in front of Jon and the other by the high-backed stool next to him. She boosted herself up onto the stool, reached in the pizza box, and lifted out a piece. She folded the thin crust like Jon had, something she'd learned to do the first week she'd been at NYU.

"This is good," Jon said.

Kate swallowed her bite. "My favorite place."

"So how'd your meeting go?" Jon took a swig of his beer and leaned back.

Meeting? Kate ran her mind back over her day. She hadn't had any meetings at work today.

"Your No Brides meeting."

"Julie left right after you did." She narrowed her eyes. "What did Ava tell you?"

"That you and five or six of your professional friends get together once a week and plot your takeover of corporate America."

Kate laughed, partially out of relief. That was a lot better than what she thought Ava might have said.

Jon placed his beer on the bar. "And that you all arm

yourselves against the wicked men who might impede your professional progress by luring you into a relationship, or worse, marriage." He wiggled his eyebrows in a villainous way that would have made her laugh if it didn't make her so sad her sister saw her ambition that way.

"Ava told you that?"

"More or less." He smiled.

"She doesn't have it exactly right. We're not anti-marriage or anti-men."

"That's good."

Kate couldn't decipher the relief that replaced the hurt of Ava's take on her and the No Brides Club that she'd given Jon. But she welcomed it.

"We each have certain career goals we want to achieve and until we do, we're putting our careers first." *Except four of the group seemed to have forgotten their joint vow. And the jury was out on Julie's suspicious need to leave tonight before they'd even gotten started.* Change that "before they'd even gotten started" to before she could let loose with her past two weeks since Jon had started at DeBakker.

"I used to be like that, and I can still say that I've never let a woman interfere with my career."

Kate finished her pizza. "Then you understand. Ava is so starry-eyed in love with Trey that she can't fathom why I don't want the same with someone."

"You don't?"

"Not now. I thought you got that when you said you never let a woman get in the way of your career."

"True, but you might say I let my grandfather interfere."

"That's different. He's family, and he was sick. Besides you already were a manager."

"Who says I didn't want more?"

"Did you?"

Jon polished off his beer. "No, I was ready for something else."

Without thinking, Kate playfully punched him in the shoulder and pulled her arm back quickly when she realized what she'd done.

"So you were doing what you wanted with your career."

"Pretty much."

"That's what my friends and I want to do."

"Be sure." Jon reached for another slice of pizza.

"I am. Sure. Do you want another beer?"

"No, I'm good."

Kate slid off the stool, walked around Jon's end of the bar and got herself another beer, feeling Jon's gaze on her back nearly the whole way. Or was it that she wanted his gaze on her. She swung the refrigerator door closed and stared at its chrome finish. She was *not* getting this close to her dream and letting whatever her attraction to Jon was get in the way.

She spun around and, while walking the few steps back to her stool, came up with a way to push Jon back into his coworker, subordinate compartment. "I told you about my No Brides Club, tell me about your competitive swimming. Is that how you came out of your shell?"

Jon shrugged. "I always liked swimming, and when I was at Columbia-Greene Community College, the athletics department was trying to get a team going. Anyone who tried out made the team."

"Wait. I'm confused. You're at Columbia-Greene now."

"When I was a student there."

Kate went still, the beer bottle halfway to her lips. "You went to community college? I know Genesee is a small high school, but you were valedictorian. Weren't you accepted at every university that had a math program?"

Jon held her gaze without answering until she had to look down.

"Yes. But my parents refused to help me with college if I didn't go pre-med. If I had, they would have paid for everything. So I moved in with Grandpa and used money I'd saved as a kid from birthday and Christmas gifts from my other grandparents to go to CGCC for the first two years."

"That's why you made such a big deal about the Mathletes scholarship. You weren't just being spiteful." Kate bit her tongue. If anyone had been spiteful, it had been her... lording her higher score over him.

"I was so angry. I had the higher math average. I was the more dedicated student."

That wasn't exactly true. She'd downplayed her scholastic diligence for popularity. Kate's chest tightened. She'd had a good financial aid package. Maybe if she'd known Jon's situation she wouldn't have worked so hard to beat him out of the scholarship ... Kate hung her head. *No.* She'd been such a fake and princess then.

"With part-time work, an academic scholarship, and student loans, I finished my bachelor's degree at Boston College and had a fellowship for my masters."

His voice had an underpinning of pride and of steel that she never would have expected from the old Jon.

John crushed his napkin in his hand and dropped it on his plate. "But you asked about my competitive swimming."

His subject change was so definite that her apology for her high-school self died on her lips. "Yes," she said too enthusiastically. "And the butterfly that emerged from it." Had she really just called him a butterfly? She stuffed the last of her pizza in her mouth before anymore words could get out. But he *was* gorgeous.

"If you mean, I lost weight and built muscle, yeah. I

swam for Boston College, too, and swim with the Dolphins Masters club now."

"I'd like to see you swim sometime."

Jon's eyes brightened. "How about this weekend. We have a home meet at Hyde Park. You can meet my grandfather."

She swallowed hard. She'd kind of been making small talk, subconsciously thinking that would flatter him. Maybe she hadn't evolved as much since high school as she thought.

"Sure." She didn't have any specific weekend plans and wasn't about to lie.

Jon rose. "I should get going."

Kate walked him to the door. "See you tomorrow. At work."

She stared at the closed door for a while before locking it behind Jon. She'd just agreed to spend the weekend watching Jon swim, after agreeing last Sunday to spend another weekend sometime visiting his grandfather's farm. What had she been thinking?

Kate turned the door lock and snapped the deadbolt into place. Her bigger problem was that despite not knowing for sure that he wasn't after her promotion, she was looking forward to both.

CHAPTER 7

*H*ad he really asked Kate, his boss, to come and watch him compete in a swim meet tomorrow? What was he, 17-years-old again? As soon as the invitation was out of his mouth, he knew that she'd just been making conversation, didn't actually want to come to the meet. And all the stuff he'd spilled about putting himself through school. He didn't tell anyone that.

"Do you have the revised projection?" Gregg, the fund manager he was working with on the special project stood in the doorway to the small conference room Jon was working in.

"I have a revised projection, based on what you asked for at the meeting this morning." A meeting that as far as Jon could see, Gregg had required his attendance at simply because he could. The meeting had had nothing to do with the minor fixed income element he was working on, and Gregg had already asked him for the same revisions late yesterday afternoon. Jon scrutinized the numbers on his screen again. But, if he hadn't had the early morning meeting, he wouldn't have had pizza with Kate last night.

"Email me the report." Gregg turned to leave.

"As soon as I run my assumptions by Kate or the fixed-income senior analyst. This is outside my area of expertise."

Gregg turned back and stepped into the conference room. "That's what they get for having you train under a woman. Given your background, I expected you to be more decisive. Especially, if you want the open fund manager position."

Jon almost lost it, but it wouldn't do anyone any good if he let his anger take over. "There you go. I don't want the fund manager position. What I want is to learn as much and do the best I can as a junior analyst for the twelve weeks Bob hired me for. I'll send you the report after I consult with Kate."

"Fine." Gregg left.

Jon closed his laptop and headed toward Kate's cubicle. He was 99% sure he'd used the correct assumptions, but Gregg had rubbed him the wrong way from the start of the project Monday afternoon. The closer he got to Kate's cubicle, the more hesitant he felt. He wouldn't want *her* to see him as indecisive professionally. He could consult the fixed income senior analyst. It wouldn't matter what he might think.

"Jon."

"Kate." He almost walked right into her. Not only was he indecisive, he was getting downright spacey.

"Done with the project?"

"Almost. I'm working on 30-, 90-, and 180-day projections for fixed income instruments and want an expert's validation of my core assumptions."

"Kim's analyst is on vacation, so you'll have to make do with me."

"Just the expert I was thinking of. Give me a time."

"Now's fine. Grab your chair and set up your laptop in my cubicle. I'm going to get a refill on my coffee, but I'll be right back."

Jon pulled his chair in next to Kate's, opened his laptop on her desk and punched in his password. His spreadsheet flashed onto the screen. As far as he could tell, it was perfect. Maybe Gregg was right. He didn't need a second opinion. But it was Kate he'd primarily be working with while he was here. Jon ignored the uptick in his pulse that anticipation evoked. He half smiled at the exasperated but determined look on her face last night when she corrected any misinformation her sister might have given him about her No Brides Club. He never knew what to expect from her.

"Is the screensaver that riveting?" Kate placed her coffee mug on the desk.

"I was lost in thought."

"I know, a mathematical challenge can do that to me, too."

His challenge wasn't numbers. It was the woman sitting next to him. Jon tapped the spacebar, and his spreadsheet was back. He summarized his task and waited.

Kate reviewed the spreadsheet, using her financial calculator to double check his results. "I would have set up the spreadsheet a little differently, but gotten the same results."

"How would you have set it up?" he asked.

Kate explained, ending with "totally a personal preference."

He'd thought his results were spot on, but didn't begrudge the time spent with Kate, having her confirm them. In fact he kind of liked times like this, working closely with her as a team. He'd miss them when his summer stint was over.

"But if Gregg doesn't need your input immediately," Kate

continued, "I have new data on short-term interest rates that you might want to substitute for the data you have here."

"Sure."

"I'll email it to you."

Jon took that as his cue to leave. He closed his laptop and stood.

"And Jon." Kate looked up.

He waited.

"Good luck with the project."

He had no idea why her words deflated rather than boosted him. What had he expected? Jon stepped across the walkway to his cubicle, sat, and opened his laptop. He hadn't firmed up his invitation to the swim meet tomorrow. There was only one way to find out if she'd been making idle conversation when she'd said she'd like to see him compete. Ask.

He swiveled his chair around to see Kate hustle out of her cubicle, laptop in hand. Probably a meeting. At the private equity firm, they joked that their jobs were 50% work and 50% meetings. He'd catch her later, or let her check with him about the swim meet. If she didn't by the end of the work day, he'd know she'd had no intention of coming.

His stomach muscles clenched. Begging for a second opinion on his work was bad enough. This was worse. He was falling back into those old patterns, sliding into the insecure adolescent who'd hidden behind his nerdiness. He was letting his old puppy love cloud his adult reality. Kate was just a friend, a coworker. Who knew if they'd even stay in contact after his work here was done? Jon slapped the desktop. As soon as she was back, he'd take the initiative. He'd tell her he was fine with her not coming to his swim meet.

His insides went from clenched to knotted, and the two of them in the elevator of her building flashed in his mind.

He wanted her to come.

"Kate, Anthony, I need you both to stay a minute," Bob said at the end of the weekly analyst meeting

"Certainly." Her colleagues shot her alternately pitying and jealous looks as they left the conference room. She glanced at the clock on the wall. 11:35. She had a noon appointment with a mortgage broker about financing the purchase of her apartment. She'd made it at lunchtime so she wouldn't have to take any time off work.

Anthony took his time moving closer to where she and Bob sat.

"How did the switching of your assistants this week work out?" Bob asked.

"I ... I," Kate and Anthony spoke at once, he continuing when Kate paused for Bob to give one of them the floor and kicking herself for doing so.

"Frankly, for all of his credentials, I wasn't impressed with Jon. We were at the edge of our deadline when he told Gregg he needed further validation of his results and wasted time making unnecessary updates in his data. All the way through the project, he questioned me."

Kate wondered if Anthony was criticizing Jon's thoroughness because it delayed the final report slightly or because he saw Jon as a threat. The other senior analyst had made it no secret he wanted a fund manager position—any fund—as David DeBakker had made it no secret at the other meeting last week that he wanted to hire Jon permanently.

"I disagree," she said. "I find Jon's thoroughness and questions about the how and why about our procedures, assumptions, and decisions a positive." And she'd take his methodical approach to management over her temporary assistant's know-it-all attitude. The woman went plunging ahead without asking questions, and forcing Kate to redo half her work.

"It was you he went to for verification," Anthony said, as if accusing her of some misdoing. "Not the fixed-income fund analyst."

"Yes, it was. And ..." she addressed Bob. "I found Hana difficult to work with. We have different work styles." Knowing the difficult career path women had here and at other mutual fund companies, Kate saw no reason to voice other criticism of her temporary assistant, unless specifically asked. She glanced at the clock again. Her appointment time was getting close.

"Anything else?" Bob asked.

"I assume now that the special project is finished, Jon is back with the Growth and Income Fund team," Kate said.

"Yes," Bob answered.

Kate rose and left, with Anthony on her heels.

"You don't get it, do you?" he asked as they stepped into the hall.

"Pardon?" She really needed to get to her appointment, but couldn't help asking.

"Cozying up to the competition isn't the way to get ahead here, especially when you're in the senior position."

Kate turned on him. "Whatever are you talking about?"

"The Briarwood Tavern."

"What about it?"

"Your little tete-a-tete.

Kate steeled herself.

"HR might be interested in it."

Not unless Jon tendered a complaint, which was ridiculous. "I have a noon appointment to make."

It took everything Kate had not to storm away, and she was shaking by the time she reached her cubicle to grab her purse. DeBakker discouraged office relationships in general, but only boss-subordinate relationships, like hers and Jon's, were technically against company policy. Only she and Jon didn't have a personal relationship. And even if he wanted one—which she was sure he didn't—hadn't she made it perfectly clear last night that she didn't? She winced. After he'd almost kissed her. Or she'd imagined he was going to kiss her. Jon wasn't even here and he had her flustered. Not what she needed when she had to convince a mortgage broker to consider her potential to exceed the financial requirements for a mortgage to buy her apartment and not just her almost-there financial situation.

Forty minutes later, Kate walked out of the bank buoyed by the fact that the broker said she'd take all of the information Kate had provided under advisement in her recommendation to the underwriting group.

"Kate," Jon came up the sidewalk from behind her. "I was looking for you before I left for lunch."

She refused to entertain that the warmth she'd felt at Jon's words was anything more than a carryover of her happiness about getting things rolling to buy her apartment.

"What's up?"

Jon fell into step with her on the side closest to the street. "I'm all yours."

Kate stumbled, and Jon took her elbow.

As much as she admired and appreciated his gallantry, she didn't want to give him the wrong idea. "Uneven crack in the sidewalk." She straightened her arm, and he released his hold.

"Anyway, I finished the project with Gregg's group. He appreciated the updated data, even if Anthony didn't."

"Don't I know," Kate mumbled.

"Pardon?"

"I had a meeting this morning with him and Bob." Kate took a deep breath and let it out. "He, Anthony that is, thinks you did the extra work to show off because you want the Growth and Income Fund Manager position."

Jon shook his head. "Maybe I should wear a sign, *Temporary Employee: Leaving August 1.*"

Kate laughed half-heartedly. She was as bad as her colleagues. She couldn't shake the small suspicion that the man doth protest too much. They walked the next half-block in silence.

"About my swim meet tomorrow ..."

A good opening to talk to him about limiting their relationship strictly to work.

Jon's voice dropped. "Don't feel like you have to come."

He didn't want her to come? She *had* invited herself. An almost imperceptible slump in his broad shoulders reminded her of the old Jon, the one she owed for all her evilness in high school.

"Of course I plan to come."

"WHEN GRANDPA GETS UP, tell him I'm out checking on the new calf Gavin saw this morning when he rotated the herd to the far field. I'll be right back in for supper, which"—Jon breathed in the delicious aroma of Dottie's cooking and his stomach growled—"smells wonderful."

"He's up, then?" she asked. "He's been *resting* since three after trekking out to check that calf himself after lunch."

"He didn't take the ATV?"

"No, you know how he feels about it."

"Yeah, an expletive menace to Mother Nature and the tranquility of the country," as his grandfather had frequently reminded him since he'd bought the vehicle the week Grandpa had come home.

The kitchen screen door swung closed behind Jon with a bang, and he headed toward said vehicle parked next to the barn, his Australian shepherd, Barney, joining him, tail wagging. Like his grandfather, he bypassed the vehicle in favor of walking. He needed to work off the inactivity of the more-crowded-than-usual train ride home, and the remarks Anthony had made on Jon's way out of the office.

Jon kicked a small rock out of his path, and Barney bounded after it. The remarks had begun with "good luck with the ice queen." It hadn't taken a lot of brain power to figure out Anthony meant Kate. Nor a lot of testosterone to want to punch the guy in the face. Barney ran back to him and dropped the rock by his feet. Jon picked it up and threw it with all his strength. Anthony had followed that with a warning to him not to think he had the fund manager opening in the bag because of what Dave DeBakker had said at last week's meeting. According to Anthony, *they*, whoever they were, liked to keep people on their toes.

Barney dropped the rock at his feet again with a woof. Jon heaved it again. The two minutes Jon had taken to hear Anthony's drivel and getting through a crowd clogging the sidewalk because of a construction scaffolding that hadn't been there this morning, had made Jon miss his usual train. The combination of that and the frustrations of walking the line between wanting to know Kate better personally and possibly jeopardizing her career, had him wondering if the summer gig at DeBakker was worth it.

The heifer that had birthed this morning hadn't had any problems, and Dottie's grandson had spotted her right off and stayed with her. But Jon couldn't help thinking he should have been there instead. This was his, and Grandpa's, operation and more valuable in the long run than what he was learning at DeBakker. Even though he was learning a lot. *And then there was Kate.*

Jon looked at the red-orange sun sitting just above the horizon. There was no way he could deny that something was going on between them, something he wanted to see out to its conclusion, even if that meant just getting her out of his system. That conclusion was unlikely to happen if he left now.

Barney returned without the rock and barked.

"What is it boy?"

The dog lifted his nose and barked again toward the field.

"Ah, you've found our new mother. Let's check her and the baby out."

Barney wagged his tail and walked alongside Jon.

Jon got as close as he could without spooking the cow. "Hi, Momma," he crooned, "I just want to see how you and your baby are doing." The heifer lifted her head and her nostrils twitched. Baby continued to nurse. "Looking good."

He walked a step closer and the heifer mooed a warning. He stopped and inspected the calf from where he was. He and Gavin would tag and immunize the calf once mother and baby had forged a strong bond.

"Come on, Barney." Jon turned and headed back toward the house, his earlier problems and questions overshadowed for the moment by the miracle of new life.

CHAPTER 8

Kate paid the Uber driver for the ride from the Poughkeepsie train station, at the north end of the New York Metro North line, to the Culinary Institute of America in Hyde Park, where the Masters swim meet was. She adjusted her shoulder bag before heading around to the athletics facility facing the Hudson River.

Her heart rate ticked up with each step. She slowed her pace. She'd vowed to maintain a strictly professional relationship with Jon, and then, she'd invited herself to his swim meet. Kate curled her lips in disgust. Because she'd imagined he was going to kiss her Thursday night in her apartment building elevator. When her alarm had gone off this morning, she'd toyed with not coming. But she would have needed an excuse she didn't have. Simply not showing up would have been rude, and she'd given Jon enough rude in the past.

The main building behind her, Kate saw the athletic building and her breath caught, not because of the building, but at the surrounding view. While the Hudson retained some of its beauty where it flowed past New York City into the Atlantic, parts of the mid-Hudson Valley north could take your breath away. She breathed in slowly and breathed out, the serene river view washing away most of the jitters that had been wreaking havoc with her insides. It wasn't that she never associated with her coworkers outside of the office. She'd been to holiday parties at Bob and his wife's condo and a fourth of July party at Kim's house in New Jersey.

And the No Brides Club had universally agreed that you needed to see all sides of your professional competition, know as much as you could about them. Not that Jon was competition, or at least he maintained he wasn't. But he'd been to her apartment, and the swim meet was a more neutral place to see him outside of work, more so than a weekend at his grandfather's place as Jon had suggested on their way home from their trip to Genesee. By the time Kate pulled open the glass door of the athletic facility, she'd almost convinced herself that she'd come to the meet as an extension of work, not because she had any personal interest in seeing Jon in action.

Kate followed the signs to the pool area, the strong smell of chlorine hitting her even before she stepped into the warm clammy atmosphere of the pool area itself. She spotted an empty seat at the top of the bleachers close to the door and turned in that direction before stopping herself with a silent *coward*. Jon had given her his grandfather's cell phone number, so she could text him when she arrived and he could direct her to where he was sitting. Jon had assured her it would give her a good view of the races. Somehow, sitting with Jon's grandfather struck her as too personal, too family-like. But she was sure his grandfather would be expecting her text.

She pulled out her phone.

Hi, it's Kate, Jon's friend.

What was she, 10? She deleted *Jon's friend*.

I'm by the door closest to the diving boards.

Dolphins' side? Jon's grandfather texted back.

How would she know? Kate's gaze darted around for another landmark and saw a man in the front row behind one of the teams rise with some effort and wave to her. She waved back. *Dolphin side*, she guessed, starting toward him, walking on the pool deck behind a few swimmers in kelly green swimsuits. She didn't see Jon, but noted the team was co-ed. Not that it mattered. She'd just assumed it was a male team.

"Kate." Jon's grandfather held his hand out to her as she approached.

"Mr. ..." She stopped. This was Jon's maternal grandfather. She had no idea what his name was.

"Pete Meyer."

"Mr. Meyer." Kate took his hand and stepped up the footrest to the first-row seat beside him.

"Pete is fine," he said, as she sat and placed her bag on the other side of her. "Glad you got here early. I didn't know how long I would be able to keep your seat for you."

She gazed around at the smattering of spectators and didn't think he would have had much of a problem with that.

"Looking for Jon?" Pete smiled, and Kate was struck by his resemblance to his grandson.

"He's warming up," the older man continued without waiting for her to answer. "Lane two, near the diving board wall."

Kate caught two powerful strokes gliding the swimmer to the wall, followed by Jon pushing himself up and out of the pool with graceful ease. Then he rose to a standing position, her mouth went dry. He was everything she'd imagined when he'd first told her about his swimming—and then some.

Beside her, Pete chuckled.

She flushed. He couldn't know what she'd been thinking. He wouldn't say anything to Jon, would he? Kate glanced sidewise at Pete, who was focused on the pool. No, he was Jon's grandfather. Grandfathers didn't talk with their grandsons about women. Did they?

"I see you found Grandpa," Jon said.

"Yes." When had he walked over? She'd been so busy playing improbable scenarios in her head that she hadn't noticed. Kate worked at keeping her gaze on his face, with a peek or two at his shoulders, chest, and biceps. Jon certainly hadn't looked like this in high school. Her gaze wandered to his abs. No one had looked like that in high school.

"The meet will get going soon, so I need to get back to the team."

She jerked her gaze up, and caught a hint of self-satisfied male in his smile before he turned to leave. She clenched her hands into fists on her lap. Jon had known she was ogling him and had liked it. Kate unfurled her fingers. She'd liked what she'd seen, too.

"Did Jon warn you that these meets can be boring? I usually bring a book to fill the time between his events."

"He warned me. I have my tablet to do some work I brought with me. Do you often come to his meets?"

"As often as I can. He's my only grandchild and I didn't see him much when he was growing up. The farm was dairy then. It was hard for me to get coverage so I could get away. Callie, my wife, would go without me."

"I know what you mean. My parents have a dairy farm."

"Right. Jon told me and that you left at 18 and never looked back."

Kate bristled inside. She reminded herself that she was talking to an elder, Jon's grandfather—who apparently, Jon did talk to about her. "I wouldn't say that. I went to NYU and found that city life fit me better than country life."

"Jon thought that, too. Then ..."

The sound system came on with the announcement of the first race, and Pete never finished his thought.

Out of the corner of her eye, Kate studied his profile, so like Jon's. Or maybe he had finished by implication. Jon had chosen to work in Boston, and then had come back to help his grandfather.

She watched the swimmers lining up on the starting blocks for the first race, one Jon wasn't competing in. She wasn't so sure Jon couldn't be just as comfortable in the city.

Or maybe she hoped he could be.

JON SURFACED from his dive into the pool for his last event, the final of the freestyle relay, to the familiar rush of sound echoing off the tiled walls. He imagined Kate's voice was in the sound, which cost him a nanosecond of time he didn't have. He blanked out her imagined cheering and put his all into the race. His team was depending on him to close the gap between them and the opposing relay team now in first place. At the last turn, he pushed ahead but with every breath could see his competition in the adjacent lane breathing down his neck. He drew on muscle reserve he didn't know he had and touched the finish wall, feeling more than seeing his closest competitor almost right with him.

Jon lifted his head out of the water and locked gazes with Kate. She lifted her hand in a victory sign and his pounding heart pounded harder.

"Good swim," a deep voice beside him said.

Jon yanked his gaze away, catching his personal best time as he turned to nod to the guy beside him, who'd come in second.

"You, too," Jon said with sincere admiration. The guy was older, probably had 20 years on him. He'd been surprised the opposing team had him swimming anchor, the position usually reserved for the fastest person on the relay team. Now he knew why. Jon wanted to be like him in 20 years.

Something inside tugged his attention back to Kate, and his thoughts went back to the elderly couple at the train station the weekend he and Kate had driven to Genesee and the conversation the two of them had had. Jon pulled himself from the pool and his teammates gathered to congratulate him. Where would he and Kate be in 20 years? Impossible to project. He didn't even know where they were now, although he had an inkling of where he wanted them to be.

The relay was his last event, but Jon stayed with the team for the rest of the meet. He and his teammates, as the host team, stood in line at the end of the meet to shake hands with the other competitors. Jon looked over to where his grandfather and Kate were sitting. His stomach flip-flopped. Or had been sitting. Only Grandpa was there now. He rolled his shoulders to shrug off his disappointment and offered a perfunctory nod to their opponents, his mind locked on Kate. She must have left to catch the train home. She'd wanted to see a meet, and she had. What more had he been expecting?

Jon headed to the locker room with the others. He'd been hoping to have dinner with Kate—and Grandpa, his mind added as an afterthought. Of course, he hadn't mentioned that to Kate. He kicked himself for the bouts of arrested development he kept suffering when it came to her. He should have invited her to dinner and to stay over at the house. He didn't like the idea of her getting into the city after dark, which it would be if they went to dinner. But since she'd apparently left, that wasn't a problem.

His heart seesawed back up when he exited the locker room and found Grandpa *and* Kate waiting for him.

"I took the liberty of asking Kate to eat with us," his grandfather said.

"Great. I'm starved." He'd have to do something special as a thanks to Grandpa.

"How about that steak place we went to in Rhinebeck the last time," Grandpa said.

"The Coach House," Jon said. He made a quick comparison between the Briarwood and the historic Coach House tavern. "Good choice. But, Kate, you'll have to take Amtrak rather than the Metro home."

"I offered to put her up at the farm," Grandpa said.

Score another point for Grandpa.

"I'm okay with taking Amtrak from the Rhinebeck Station," she said

His grandfather shook his head. "I don't like it. A woman alone at Penn Station after dark." He looked toward Jon as if inviting his support.

As much as he wanted to lend support to Grandpa's invitation Kate, something in the way she'd set her jaw when his grandfather had said "a woman" stopped him.

"We're over there, the other side of the green pickup," he said. The trio walked to Jon's vehicle.

Three hours later, they walked out of the Coach House toward the car again. Jon had forgotten how busy the restaurant was on Saturday night. But Kate hadn't appeared bothered about their wait for a table, and the food, service, and dinner company had been stellar. At least as far as Jon was concerned.

Kate's phone pinged as she settled into the front seat with him. Grandpa had insisted he'd be more comfortable in the back seat. A good man to have on his side, if he could figure out what his side was.

She dug in her bag for her phone. "I have to check it." She apologized. "I have it on do not disturb, so this has to be an important exception to ring through."

"Work?" He failed to stop the twist his lips took. He'd been doing his best to keep today strictly personal—two friends enjoying themselves—and didn't want any reminders of their work relationship changing that.

"No, my travel app."

She wrinkled her nose accenting the freckles sprinkled across it and resurrecting his age-old desire to kiss her that simmered beneath his controlled surface.

"Something wrong?" he asked.

"You could say that. A freight train derailed just north of Poughkeepsie. Neither Amtrak nor the Metro will be running for hours."

The corners of Jon's mouth twitched. He would *not* grin, although a grin would be better than his other inclination: to shout *woohoo*. Kate would have to take his grandfather up on his invitation to stay at the farm.

"My app recommends the Rhinebeck Village Inn as a hotel

that has rooms available tonight." At a price that was enough to make a dent in Kate's carefully budgeted spending money for the month. "Do you know it? Is it a decent place?"

"I won't hear of it," Jon's grandfather said from the back seat. "If Jon and I hadn't talked you into having dinner with us, you would have been on your way home before the derailment. You'll stay with us."

Jon's face ran such a gamut of expressions at his grandfather's proclamation, that she was tempted to pull out her phone and record him. "Is your grandfather always so, uh …" She didn't want to be disrespectful. "So direct?"

"Yes, he's always this bossy," Jon said with a laugh.

"Harrumph." Jon's grandfather cleared his throat in the back seat.

"It's one of the things I love about Grandpa. You always know where you stand with him."

Unlike his grandson. Kate folded and unfolded her hands in her lap. Or maybe she wasn't being fair. Jon had made it clear in words more than once that he didn't want a permanent position—the fund manager position she wanted—and hadn't said anything to indicate he was attracted to her. She assigned those positive assumptions to the equation herself.

"Stop at the chain drugstore in Red Hook and go in and get Kate whatever she needs to get through until tomorrow," Jon's grandfather said.

Kate looked over her shoulder at Pete. "I would like to pick up a few things, but I'll pay for them." She'd be more comfortable if Jon didn't come in the store with her. Silly as it might be, the idea of Jon buying her a toothbrush and other personal grooming items struck her as too intimate.

"You wouldn't have to buy them if we didn't talk you into having dinner with us," Pete replied.

Jon just shook his head.

"He can afford it," Pete said.

As if she couldn't? What part of her being Jon's boss hadn't his grandfather caught?

"You're saving your money to buy your apartment," Pete added.

Jon had told his grandfather that? The smaller but still lingering doubts she still had about swinging the apartment deal rose to the surface, along with her brother's old taunt *only a girl* to which Kate's doubts added *versus Jon being a man and, by default, better able to pay*. She wouldn't be buying anything she wouldn't eventually have to buy anyway. Kate bit her tongue hard. She didn't want to be disrespectful.

Jon pulled into the drug store parking lot. She'd settle this with Jon, privately, on their walk into the store. He got out and walked around to her door, which she opened quickly before he could. She stepped out and noted, to Jon's favor, that he let her close the door. Well, didn't *let* her, just didn't reach over and shut it for her. She shook her head. Maybe she was taking her *I am woman, hear me roar* too far.

"I know," Jon said, misconstruing her head shake. "There's no arguing with him. If he checks the debit card—our joint account—I'll tell him it's against company policy for me to buy my boss gifts other than the allowable holiday gift exchanges? It is, isn't it?"

Jon's lopsided grin shot right through her, intensifying the already warm feelings his respect for her as an equal had ignited.

"I'll wait for you here." Jon stepped over to the book rack on the other side of the checkout and away from any view his grandfather would have from the car.

"Thanks. And, yes, bribing your boss with personal hygiene gifts has to be against company policy." Kate did nothing to restrain the bounce in her step, nor did she try to figure out why she was getting such a kick out of her and Jon's little conspiracy against his well-meaning grandfather.

Kate giggled when she approached the checkout with her things and Jon moved so that he would be blocking any view his grandfather might have of her paying the cashier. He opened the door for her and followed her out of the store, walking her to the car and opening the passenger side door for her with a muted, "I can't have grandpa lecturing me on my manners as a gentleman."

"Certainly not," Kate agreed.

"Did you get everything you needed?" Pete asked.

"Yes, I did." *And then some*, she added to herself, remembering how Jon's intuitive treatment had warmed her. She swallowed hard. Jon's thoughtfulness as an adult wasn't any different than his thoughtfulness in high school. Back then, she and her group had seen it as weak and nerdy. She pretended to be looking at the scenery out of the car window to hide the heat that flamed her cheeks.

"Our place is on the next road." Pete broke the silence in the car.

"I'm looking forward to seeing it. When Jon told me about the farm on our trip to Genesee, he invited me to come up some weekend and see it."

"He did, did he?"

Kate heard the speculation in Pete's voice and resituated herself in her seat. First, Ava thinking they were a couple. Now, Jon's grandfather thinking ... whatever he was thinking. They were coworkers. Jon was no more than that. Maybe a friend. Yeah, a friend. A friend she'd kept thinking about kissing ever since the night they'd had pizza at her apartment.

Jon pulled up a tree-lined driveway to a house that reminded her of her parents' house.

"My wife and I planted those trees as a wind and snow barrier the summer we bought the farm," Pete said as he climbed out of the car. "Only lost one, the winter my daughter was born."

From what Jon had told her about his family, Kate wasn't going to touch the latter part of the older man's statement.

Jon stepped in to break the awkward silence. "You guys go ahead into the house. I'm going to take care of the evening chores before it's fully dark. Let Barney out to help me."

"Good with me," his grandfather said. "I'm bushed and won't be much company. Take Kate with you, too. Show her the place, what we do."

Jon rolled his eyes at his grandfather's back. "You don't have to come if you don't want to. I'm just going to check the pasture the herd is in and the water source, make sure they haven't gummed up the flow to the trough." He patted the head of the shepherd that had joined them, tail wagging. "It's not like you haven't seen cows before."

She laughed. "That's an understatement." But she hadn't seen *his* cows. "It's a nice night and after that dinner I could use a walk around. Besides, I think your grandfather may have had enough socializing for the day."

"Probably. We have a new calf. If we don't spot her tonight, we can walk out tomorrow morning and check on her. That is, if you want to."

Kate would have had to be totally disconnected from Jon —which she wasn't given how he'd affected her earlier—to miss the excitement in his voice when he'd mentioned the calf.

"Sounds like a plan." She smiled. "I always liked the babies. It was just when they got bigger, I could do without them and the work we all had to pitch in on. Although evening chores that consist of just checking the pasture and water are a lot better than all that has to be done afternoon and evening with a contained dairy herd."

"Why do you think I talked Grandpa into selling off the Holsteins?"

"So you wouldn't have to do dairy chores."

"Smart woman."

"Smart man." On impulse Kate lifted her hand and Jon high-fived her. From the way he'd jerked his hand away, she wasn't the only one who'd felt a jolt of electricity at their touch. He shifted his weight from foot to foot. There was definitely something going on between them. It was the 21st century. If Jon wasn't going to take the initiative to find our what, she was.

While he was still immobilized from the current of their pressed palms, Kate stepped forward, rose on her toes, and pressed her lips to his. If she'd thought their high-five had packed a jolt, it was nothing compared to the bone-melting charge that the touch of their lips was sending through her.

Before she could ground herself, Jon pulled her tight to him and continued what she'd started, tentatively at first, then deepening it to the point where her world was shrunk to him and her.

Sooner than she wanted, Jon gently ended the kiss and disentangled them. "I ... uh ... the chores."

Kate's heart soared. This was *her* endearing, nerdy Jon. She stepped back from the intense emotion that thought evoked in her. She knew who Jon was, but who was she? His friend? His boss? The consummate professional? The small-town girl she'd escaped from being?

"I ... yes, the chores. You go ahead. I forgot I bought creamer. The flavored kind I like in my coffee," she stammered. "At the drugstore. On the hood of the car. In the bag. It needs to be refrigerated."

She fled before she sounded any more insane, holding one thought in her mind and heart.

So, that's what kissing Jon was like.

Jon had spent too much of his high school days wondering what it would be like to kiss Kate. None of that speculation had come close to reality. A reality that was imprinted on his brain as clearly this morning as it had been when he'd come in last night from chores to find both Kate and his grandfather retired to their rooms. The combination of relief and disappointment that had struck him had been staggering.

But what had he expected? Kate to meet him at the door ready to pick up where they'd left off in the pasture? Her awkward escape from him should have told him firmly *no*. Although she had initiated the kiss, he hadn't had to let his hormones override his reason. She was his boss, even if only temporarily, and his friend. He didn't know in what order. Not that it mattered. He didn't want to mess up either relationship.

He put on the coffee and whistled softly to Barney to come outside with him and move the herd to today's pasture. Once he had the cattle moved, Jon surveyed today's pasture. If they didn't get a good soaking rain soon, he'd have to supplement their grass grazing with hay. He double checked the latch on the gate. Maybe he should haul out a bale this morning. What was he thinking? The herd didn't need hay today. He just wanted to delay facing Kate.

"You're just in time for pancakes," his grandfather said when Jon stepped into the kitchen. "I'm not much for cooking, but I do make a mean pancake."

Jon let go of the screen door. It closed behind him with a click. Grandpa wasn't talking to him. Kate had entered the kitchen from the dining room at the same time.

"It all smells so good, but I need coffee first."

"You can thank Jon for that."

Their gazes locked over the kitchen table that separated them, Kate breaking the connection to take the coffee mug his grandfather was offering.

Jon walked over to the refrigerator, opening the door and holding it open while he studied Kate from the back as she filled the mug. Something was different about her. Something that had nothing to do with their kiss. She turned around and he ducked his head into the appliance. He was an idiot. A besotted idiot? The same besotted idiot he'd been in high school? All that was different was that her hair was down, rather than pulled back and up or in a fancy braid.

He righted himself and closed the refrigerator. "Here's that creamer you were concerned about last night."

Kate's eyes widened and his grandfather frowned at him.

Jon had his answer. He was the same besotted idiot he'd been as a teenager. And, at the moment, he didn't feel any better equipped to deal with it than he had then.

"Thanks," she said.

"I'll put it on the table," *and shut up*, Jon said. Anyone seeing him now would never believe he'd dated an up-and-coming super model for a while. A woman who didn't hold a candle to Kate. He waited until Kate had sat at the table before walking around it to fill another mug with his coffee. Before he turned around with his coffee, he decided he was safest sitting next to her at the four-seat table, rather than across where he'd be directly facing her.

His grandfather placed a plate with a stack of pancakes and sausage links on the table in front of the two of them. Jon took a long gulp of coffee to allow her to get her breakfast first. He watched her over the rim. After her initial reaction to his coffee creamer comment, she appeared to be perfectly comfortable sitting next to him, digging into her breakfast.

He forked a couple of pancakes and sausages onto his plate and smothered them in butter and maple syrup. She'd been upset after the kiss last night, couldn't get away from him fast enough. Had she thought it over and was good with it this morning? His pulse raced at that scenario. He had no idea, and the only way to put himself out of his misery was to ask Kate.

Jon opened his mouth as his grandfather left the stove and sat in the chair on the other side of Kate. But, of course, he shouldn't ask in front of his grandfather.

Kate rested her fork on the edge of her plate. "Your grandfather said you were out moving the cows. Did you spot that new calf you told me about? I'd still like to see her, him."

"Right." The pancakes he'd eaten sat heavy in his stomach. *I'm not going to make a big deal about this.* "We can go after we finish breakfast, before I drive you to the train station."

Out of the corner of his eye, he searched her face for any indication of disappointment, that she might want to stay longer.

"Sounds good. I'd like to make the 10:30 train this morning. The track is cleared. I checked."

He swallowed the pancake he'd stopped chewing while he'd waited for her response. "Sure." Jon let his grandfather take over talking while he finished his breakfast.

Kate pushed away from the table. "That was delicious." She patted her stomach. "I really need that walk out to see the calf now. But first, let me do the dishes."

Jon glanced at the kitchen clock. Her doing the dishes would give them less time alone. "I'll give you a hand."

His grandfather waved them off. "No go ahead. I'll clean up."

"If you're sure ..."

Had Kate reconsidered? Was she looking for a way out of being alone with him?

"Go," his grandfather said.

"Come on," Jon was at the door pushing it open. He followed her down the steps. "The calf and her momma were at the near side of the pasture when I saw them earlier."

Kate looked over her shoulder at the house as if checking to see if Grandpa was watching them. "I do want to see her, but first about the elephant in the room—the kiss."

His heart sank. He hadn't been fast enough, and now Kate was in control of the conversation.

"I don't know what got into me."

He'd been rooting for a mutual attraction.

"I take full responsibility. I'm your boss. It won't happen—"

"Don't," he interrupted. "Don't deny that there's something going on between us."

Kate nudged a stone in the grass with the toe of her Teva. "I won't … can't. That doesn't change that I'm your boss, at least for the time being. *Nor* does it change my priorities. I'm not about to give DeBakker any reason to pass me over again for fund manager. Nor the fact that now is the wrong time for me to even think about beginning a relationship with someone, with you."

"But you don't deny the attraction."

Her voice dropped. "No, I don't." Her voice grew stronger. "But I can fight it."

"I've got a better idea." Jon couldn't believe he was saying this. "Why don't we be friends, that's all, until August, when I go back to teaching. No promises. No strings."

Her nose wrinkled and she pursed her lips as she used to when she was working out a challenging problem at Mathletes practice.

"Yes, we can keep our relationship as friends and coworkers." Kate hesitated.

His windpipe constricted as the seconds ticked off until she continued.

"And as a friend," She grinned, "I'm going to save you from having to drive me to the train station by going back inside and calling Uber."

He stood and watched her walk away. As far as he could figure, he could take Kate's action in one of two ways. One: Despite her agreeing to friendship, she didn't want to spend the time with him. Two: Kate was afraid of where spending time alone with him might lead.

He was going with the latter.

hank God for vacations, Kate thought as she peered down the walkway to her and Jon's cubicles. Not a vacation for her, but her fellow analysts. The Monday following Jon's swim meet and *The Kiss,* Kate had had to drag her sleep-deprived self into work. She'd spent most of the day and night before working on a plan to keep a friendly distance from Jon, even though she'd have to fight her attraction to him at least eight hours a day. The only conclusion she'd come to—and one she didn't want to admit —was that her side of the attraction between her and Jon wasn't exactly just friendly. Her boss Bob had unwittingly come to her rescue with an early morning email saying he was borrowing Jon to fill in for another analyst who was on vacation.

Jon's reassignment for that week and a little strategic ducking out of her cubicle at the right times had lessened the danger of her and Jon having any one-on-one time at the office. And they hadn't had any reason to get together outside of work. Kate had made sure of that by being away from her cubicle at the time she knew Jon would be passing by on his way out to catch his train.

This week Jon had been grabbed again when another analyst had scheduled time off. And so far, so good. It was late Thursday, after Jon's usual departure time, and Kate was headed back to her cubicle to catch up on the work she was running behind on because of her ducking in and out of her work area to avoid Jon.

"Hey, there."

Kate blinked her bleary eyes. "Jon. I thought you'd be gone." *That was smooth.* But she was operating on only a few hours of sleep again last night. You would have thought she'd never been kissed before.

"Thought or hoped?" he asked.

"Thought. Why?" He must be on to her half-baked avoidance plan.

"Maybe because you've been strategically avoiding me for the past eight days. Want to catch a drink with me and talk about it? As friends."

Right. They were supposed to be friends. Kate slumped. She'd like nothing better than to go have a drink with Jon. One of her new favorites, a monster fresh cherry margarita, so she could blame any romantic entanglement she let herself get into on the alcohol. She straightened. "I had planned to stay late to catch up on work. It's been backing up without your help." *There.* She'd gotten the refusal she needed to give him out in a casual, conversational voice and complimented Jon on his work.

"What? No Brides Club meeting this evening?"

"No, everyone else cancelled." Right when she needed support—badly.

"Perfect," he said with a heart-stopping grin that set her

nerves tingling along with making her heart skip a beat or two. "I'll stand in for them."

Kate opened her mouth, but no sound came out. Tell Jon what she was going to tell her friends? That she was becoming—or already was—insanely attracted to Jon and needed help ramping down her feeling to friend-like.

An earnest expression had replaced Jon's grin.

"What the heck?" Kate raised her hands in surrender. "Let me get my bag."

"I'm not going anywhere." Jon leaned his shoulder against the cubicle support post and employed that killer smile again.

It was as if he knew what it did to her. Kate got her things from her desk drawer. He was a perceptive guy. For all she knew, he did, and perversely for someone who'd drawn the line between them at friendship, she liked that.

Feeling like a teenager skipping out of the last period at school, Kate walked out with Jon, sensing everyone's eyes on her. Hadn't anyone left for the day yet? She pulled the strap of her bag up further on her shoulder. She wasn't leaving any earlier than she did any other Thursday for the No Brides Club meeting. Her finger itched to pull her phone from her bag and text Julie or one of the other club members to...what? Talk her down? Come to her rescue by being at the Briarwood when she and Jon got there?

"And, then, I suggested we cut out the middle person and invest directly in the live elephants. What do you think?" Jon asked.

Kate stopped short and blinked at him. "Live elephants?" Jon was working with the socially responsible fund, but what was he talking about?

He opened the front door to the street, as if that's why she'd halted, and she walked into the afternoon heat. She couldn't remember the meteorologists saying so, but the recent temperatures had to be topping 100 in the heat index charts.

"You were a hundred miles away. I thought the elephants could bring you back," Jon said.

"Sorry." Why did she feel as if she were always apologizing to Jon? And what was she apologizing for? Not listening to him or being attracted to him? "I rode an elephant once," she blurted out of nowhere.

"Did you.?" He raised an eyebrow, and she tripped on another nonexistent crack in the sidewalk.

He took her elbow.

"Yes, at the county fair when I was six or seven." It was an odd conversation twist, but why not go with it to keep them talking and her mind from fixating on his touch. It was her elbow for heaven's sake. She'd tripped.

"That reminds me," Jon said. "You know how you said you'd like to come up to the farm for a weekend?

Only too well, along with the swim meet weekend.

"When we were driving home from Genesee," he prompted.

"Yeah." *Sometime next month might be good, preferably after I have my promotion to fund manager under my belt and she was one step removed from being Jon's boss. Or, even better, after that and when Jon was back to teaching full time.*

"Well." Jon's voice took on a tentative note. "Grandpa thought it might be fun to have you come for Flag Day weekend."

They were already at Briarwood. Jon opened the door for her.

She walked in. "Grandpa thought it would be fun?" Kate tossed over her shoulder, catching a sheepish look on his face.

Jon tilted his head. "I agreed with him."

"Let's go upstairs." Kate prolonged answering.

"Your usual?" Jon asked when they reached the rooftop bar.

He knew her usual? Kate wanted to fan her face.

"You can grab us a table while I get the drinks."

"Okay." She spotted an out-of-the-way table where people from work wouldn't be likely to see them. Jon was probably going to ask the bartender what her drink was. He knew she met with her No Brides Club friends here regularly. But that was thoughtful. Kate dropped into one of the two chairs at the table. What was she doing looking for more ways to like Jon. She already had too many.

Jon arrived with the drinks, a fresh cherry margarita, regular size, for her and a draft beer for him.

"I almost couldn't find you, over here in the corner." He placed the drinks on the table and sat in the other chair next to her.

His leg brushed hers. The chair was too close. She should have moved it to the other side of the table when she sat down. If anyone from work saw them here out of the way, sitting *right* next to each other they'd think ... the truth. Whether they'd admitted it or not, she and Jon were more than coworkers.

Kate lifted her margarita and took a mouthful.

"A little thirsty?" Jon teased.

"It's so warm considering it's not even officially summer yet." Kate returned the margarita glass to the table slowly.

Jon rested his leg against hers.

"No." She moved her leg and drilled her gaze into his. "It's you. Me. Us."

"You admit there's an us?" Jon almost crowed.

Kate's heart soared. Jon *did* want to be more than friends.

Hadn't he pretty much said that at the farm? But wanting didn't eliminate the boss-subordinate conflict. Her thoughts leapfrogged ahead. They'd have to keep any relationship very private until he left DeBakker.

He brushed his lips against hers as soft and fleeting as the touch of a butterfly wing. Kate went all melty inside, unable to voice a comeback, even if she could have come up with one.

She opened her eyes to Jon taking a healthy swig of his beer. Had she imagined kiss two? Kate dropped her gaze to her drink and over to his. They'd both made significant dents in their drinks.

"You just looked so cute," he said as if she'd asked him to explain his action.

He *had* kissed her. Here in public.

"I could almost hear the wheels going around in your head."

Kate breathed in and blew out the breath. "*Us* is what I was going to talk about at the No Brides Club today, if it hadn't been cancelled and how to put off any romantic *us* until we aren't working together any longer. But I'm afraid it's too late for that.

"You don't have to look like *us* being together isn't a good thing," Jon said.

She dropped her head to her chest. *I'm not certain it is a good thing.*

He reached over and lifted her chin. "We can take it slow. It's not like we just pledged our undying love to each other."

"Well, when you put it that way ..." Kate managed a wobbly smile. "We also have to keep it separate, private from work."

"Copy that." He grinned and finished his beer.

"Hey, I thought it was you guys." The greeting cut off Kate's intended reiteration of what she had at stake, giving into her and Jon's mutual attraction.

"Kim," she choked, as their fund manager coworker approached their table.

Kate finished her margarita in one slug. The No Brides Club had never let her down before. Why now when she was so close to the gold ring?

"I'd wanted to catch you before you left the office today," Kim said.

Kate tapped the side of Jon's foot with hers.

He rose. "I'd better get to the station if I want to make my train."

Relief flooded Kate. He'd read her signal.

"Right. See you tomorrow." *Now how to handle this with Kim.*

"May I?" Kim motioned to Jon's former seat.

"Sure."

Kim moved the chair 30 degrees around the table from Kate. "Bob said you usually had a meeting here after work on Thursdays."

"I do. A group of friends. Everyone else cancelled for tonight." Kate hesitated. She could say she ran into Jon, like Kim had run into them. That she'd invited him to have a drink to go over the work she had for him next week since he'd been out "on loan" to other analysts the last two weeks. But she'd never been good at stretching the truth.

"How much did you see?" Kate asked. Might as well get right to the center of things.

Kim smiled before she assumed a placid expression. "Enough."

Kate's stomach sank. She didn't know the older woman well, but had admired her professionalism.

"Don't worry," Kim added. "I don't gossip and, besides, I'm leaving DeBakker. That's what I wanted to talk to you about."

Kate moved to the edge of her seat. Kim had been with DeBakker quite a while. "Where are you going?" She respected Kim. Maybe she should put Kim's new employer on the list to check out if she didn't get her promotion.

"For starters, on a 20-day river cruise of Europe with my husband, with after-cruise stops in Paris and London. Tomorrow is my last day working at DeBakker."

Kate stared at the other woman. Kim couldn't have been fired. She would have had to pack her personal things and leave immediately.

"Technically, I'm still an employee of DeBakker for four more weeks, but I opted to take my accrued vacation and leave tomorrow."

"Wow." Kate leaned back in her chair.

"Yeah, wow." The woman stepped out of her usual subdued professional demeanor to show some excitement. "When we get back, I'm looking at some business opportunities with my husband. We've had an unexpected inherited windfall."

"Your husband is a private banker, right?"

Kim nodded as she flagged down the bar server. "I'll have a Honey Bee Brandy," she said. "Do you want another?"

"No, I'm good." She needed to keep her wits for whatever Kim was up to.

"Okay," Kim said, folding her hands on the table. "I didn't come over to interrupt your love life."

Kate winced.

"Nor was I looking for someone to gloat to about my good fortune to. If I'd wanted to, I have a couple of male colleagues, I'd descend on." Kim unfolded her hands. "What I wanted was to give you a heads-up on the additional fund manager position that's available. I have *not* recommended anyone on my current team for it. That makes a fund manager position for you and one for Jon."

"Jon's not interested in managing a fund."

Kim's wave of dismissal of Kate's declaration made her stomach churn.

"Confidentially, I can't say I've loved working at DeBakker, but it did give me an opportunity to gain the traction I wanted for my career. It could be the same for you. But if they pass you over for fund manager again, you should start looking elsewhere, if you aren't already."

"Thanks, that is my plan."

"Smart woman. Two more bits of unsolicited career advice, and then I'll back off. Be more discreet with Jon, at least until you're both at the same-level position, and don't let your career ambitions dictate the rest of your life. I've noticed how focused you are on work. That said, I wish you the best of luck with the promotion and with Jon. From the contact I've had with him, he seems like a good guy. Reminds me of my husband."

Kate thanked her and watched Kim wave to someone across the room before picking up her brandy and leaving.

She wasn't letting her career dictate the rest of her life. She had it all planned. A fund manager position was the next rung on her life-planning ladder, then buying her apartment, which was coming a little faster than planned. After that, there'd be plenty of time for other, personal goals to fall into place. Goals like love, marriage, and maybe kids.

Kate frowned at Kim's back and out of nowhere a picture of her sister Ava and Trey announcing their engagement flashed in front of her eyes. They'd looked so happy and in love, as if nothing else on earth existed but each other.

She argued down a pang of jealousy. She'd have time for that. Soon. Wouldn't she?

THE TRAIN JERKED TO A START. Jon hadn't wanted to abandon Kate, but the only way he could interpret her slapping the side of his foot with hers was as a directive to leave. So he had. It seemed simple, straight-forward enough. But he was a guy. He didn't know how women's minds worked. What if he'd read her wrong? Maybe she'd been signaling him to stay and back her up. He remembered Anthony's comment about good luck with the Ice Queen, after Anthony had seen the two of them together. Except for wanting to wipe the smirk off Anthony's face, Jon hadn't given it another thought. Personally, he didn't care what Anthony thought or about any other office rumors.

Jon tapped the news app on his phone for something to do with his hands but just stared at the media choices. His abrupt departure could make Kate look bad to Kim, like the two of them were sneaking around doing something they shouldn't be doing. Which they hadn't been, but technically might be about to if Kim's appearance hadn't changed Kate's mind. He had a good idea how much Kate's potential promotion meant to her. Too much in his opinion, but she hadn't asked his opinion. And he wouldn't give it unsolicited, even though he'd been where she was now and had found the next bump up hadn't made him any more fulfilled.

Something soft bounced over his shoulder and landed

in his lap. A multi-colored rubber ball. Jon picked it up and turned around in his seat.

"Hewo," a grinning kid, maybe two years old bounced on presumedly his mother's lap and reached for the ball Jon held in his hand.

"Hello." Jon handed the ball to the woman who also had her hand held out for it.

"Thanks, and sorry for bothering you."

"No problem." He turned around, the little boy's image still in his mind. Dark hair, big blue eyes surrounded by long dark lashes, an impish tilt to his smile. If he and Kate had a kid, he or she might look like the little guy in the seat behind him.

He'd never given much thought to having kids. He hadn't much enjoyed being a kid himself. And given his parents as an example, he didn't know if he could raise a kid. Jon scrubbed his hand down his face. He'd barely gotten Kate to agree to see him outside of work. An agreement Kate might rescind after talking with Kim. In which case, he'd have to step back. He didn't want to damage Kate's promotion prospects in any way. Jon tapped his cell phone screen and chose *The Wall Street Journal*, scrolling up to the latest article burb.

He could just leave DeBakker now, rather than August first as he'd planned. Making extra payments on the home equity loan his grandfather had taken for the barn gave the farm operation a nice financial padding. But without the extra payments, the farm was still in good financial shape. His finger itched to text Kate that, that if them seeing each other outside of work was a problem, he could quit the statistician job. Resigning should also remove him from any consideration for the fund manager position that no one at

DeBakker—including Kate, he suspected—believed he didn't want.

He flexed his finger. There was no reason to be rash. He'd talk with Kate tomorrow at work. Better yet, he'd call her tonight. Goner that he was, his pulse picked up in anticipation of hearing her voice. *Yeah*. She'd said they had to keep their relationship outside of the office.

Jon started and restarted the article on his phone three times before giving up. He could use a good swim to work off his agitation. Except the train he'd caught would get him into Hyde Park too late for practice and, contrary to what Kate thought, he didn't bring his gym bag with him everywhere, so he didn't have his swim gear with him. He shot his grandfather a text that he'd be home later than expected and got an *okay* in return.

Jon pulled into the farm driveway right at the time he'd told his grandfather to expect him. He stepped out of the car and saw the older man walk around the house from the back.

"I had to do the evening chores," his grandfather called out.

Jon swung the car door shut. "Where's Gavin?" he called back. The teen was supposed to be doing the farm chores during the workweek. That's what they'd hired him for. He strode toward his grandfather and met him at the kitchen door to the house.

His grandfather frowned. "He took your ATV out this morning to move the cattle like he couldn't just walk, and rolled it on the way back."

"Is he all right?"

"Came limping in afterwards." His grandfather continued his story. "Dottie had to run him to urgent care."

Jon tapped his foot waiting for an answer to his question.

"Might have a minor sprain or something. That's what Dottie said when she came back. He has to stay off his right foot for a couple of days."

A sign he should cut short his temporary position at DeBakker? He didn't want his grandfather rotating the herd into new grazing areas by himself. Grandpa's safety and the farm both ranked ahead of the extra money. Add Kate to the mix, and the job at DeBakker was a far fourth.

"I'll go out after supper, take a look at the ATV, and see if I can get it back up to the barn."

"No need," his grandfather said. "Dottie and I went and tipped the ATV upright and drove it back." He shook his head. "And by the way Dottie was holding on to me, you'd think she had no faith in my driving."

Jon stifled a laugh. No, he'd think something all together different. But, then, female-male attraction was the thought track he was stuck on.

The two men headed into the house and cleaned up to eat. As they were sitting down to the meal Dottie had left warming on the stove, his grandfather said, "I know it's not in the budget, but I asked Dottie to put in some extra time next week, making the place look nice for your friend's visit."

Jon stopped pulling his chair out midway. Did his grandfather think he was that much of a hard guy on finances? The budget he'd made was just his effort to get grandpa's bills and payments into some semblance of order.

"The budget is just a guide." His words came out harsher than he'd intended. "But are you sure the extra hours are necessary?'

Grandpa drew his eyebrows together.

"Or," Jon teased, "is it just a way to get Dottie to spend more time here with you?"

"I … um," Grandpa sputtered. "Impertinent brat."

Jon took his place across the table from his grandfather.

"I like your Kate." His grandfather scooped out a healthy helping of mashed potatoes and passed them to Jon.

He took the bowl. If only she were *his* Kate. Jon took half the helping his grandfather had. He'd settle for a positive possibility she someday *could* be.

"So is Kate coming Friday after work or Saturday morning? Friday is better. The Flag Day parade starts early on Saturday."

Jon placed the serving spoon back in the bowl. "I don't know. We didn't get around to talking about it.

"Wasn't that why you got home late. You were talking with Kate?"

'Yeah, but …"

"But what? It's simple enough. You ask her if she wants to go to the Flag Day celebration with us. She says yes or no. If she says yes, you set a time."

Jon rocked back in his chair. If only it were that easy.

CHAPTER 10

The next morning Kate turned the corner from Murray Street onto Broadway, still buoyed by Kim's news about leaving DeBakker and opening up another fund manager position. With two positions up for grabs, it didn't matter if Jon did want to stay on at DeBakker. In fact, it could be good for feeling out their relationship, seeing where it could lead. Some people might find the intrigue of being discreet exciting, but she wasn't crazy about having to watch where and when they could be seen together. And the discrepancy in their superior-subordinate status would be even wider if she were to be promoted to fund manager this summer while he was an assistant statistician. *Yes.* She nodded. It would be good if they were both fund managers. That is, if that's what Jon wanted.

"Kate."

She halted at the corner of Park Place. That sounded like Jon. But what would he be doing here, blocks from work?

"Wait up."

She blinked at the figure jogging up Park toward her. Her pulse raced. It *was* Jon.

"What are you doing here?" she blurted when he reached the corner. *Nice way to greet him.*

"I got off at the Park Place subway station, hoping to catch you on your walk to work. I need to ask you something."

"Me, too. I mean I want share to some good news about work, something Kim told me."

"My question doesn't have anything to do with work."

Jon's words warmed her more than they should.

He stepped to the street side of the sidewalk, his arm brushing hers while people walked around them. "Shall we?" He motioned forward.

Kate glanced around them, remembering Kim's caution. If any coworkers saw them walking to work from so near her apartment, they might get the wrong idea, and conclude that they were both walking *from* her apartment. Not that she'd ever run into any coworkers at this point on her daily walk to work.

Satisfied no one she knew would see them she stepped in line with Jon. "You first."

"Okay. You didn't answer my question about Flag Day."

Flag Day. Her mind blanked for a second. She'd gotten so caught up in her conversation with Kim, she'd forgotten all about Jon's invitation.

"Coming for the weekend to go to the parade and stuff with Grandpa and me. My text last night."

"No, I ..." Jon's breaking eye contact with her stopped Kate short. She cleared her throat. "I meant no, I didn't get your text."

Jon pulled out his phone and rolled his eyes in an expression that was so adorable she wanted to squeeze him.

"I sent the text to the wrong person. Someone at my dentist's office is probably wondering why I was inviting them to the Flag Day parade." He gave her a sheepish look. "I replied to the appointment reminder I got before your text.

Kate burst out laughing.

"So, what do you say?" he asked.

Her mind did a quick replay of Kim's admonishment about career ambitions overshadowing her personal life. "Yes, I'd love to come this weekend."

The Flag Day celebration was Upstate, near Jon's grandfather's farm ... Jon's farm, too ... She couldn't think of anyone from work who lived near there. It would give her and Jon time together without worry about someone from DeBakker seeing them.

"All right," he said.

The grin of pure joy Jon flashed her made Kate want to throw all caution to the wind and go full-speed ahead on exploring a relationship with him, which she'd be able to do once she had her promotion in hand.

"Next question. Do you want to come this evening after work or tomorrow morning? The parade is in the morning. That's why I took an earlier train today and waylaid you on your way to work."

Kate wasn't quite following.

"If you want to come today, I can cover for you at the office if you want to take a long lunch to go home and pack or leave early to pack and meet me at Penn Station."

"Thanks for the offer." Kate bit her lower lip. She was hesitant to shave any work time off her day. "How early in the morning is the parade?"

"Nine. Grandpa wants to leave the house around eight to get to Hudson, where the parade is, and find a good viewing spot on the parade route."

"Eight *is* early." She'd have to catch a train out of the city at about 6 am, if Amtrak even ran north that early on the weekend. "What train do you usually take home?"

"Usually, the 5:47. Sometimes the 4:40."

Kate calculated how much time she'd need to get home and pack for a couple days. Fortunately, she'd done laundry Wednesday night. "I can do it, if I get out of the office no later than 4:30."

That would be better than running home and back at lunch time and walking out of the office with Jon and an overnight bag. Sometime this weekend, she'd need to talk with Jon about keeping their private life, such that it was, out of the office.

"Great. We can meet at the Chamber Street Subway station near your apartment and go to Penn Station together."

She'd been thinking of meeting at Penn Station, where they'd be less likely to run into anyone from work. Kate nibbled her lower lip again, stopping when she caught Jon studying her, his eyes darkening. She shook off the rush his perceived interest caused.

"That would be fine. About 5:15? On the platform?"

"Sounds good." Jon reached for the plate glass door of their office building.

"Good morning."

Kate started at the booming voice and turned to see Anthony materialize right behind her.

"`Morning." She slipped through the doorway to their coworker's, "I thought it was you two walking up the street."

Kate cringed. Good decision on packing her overnight bag after work. As far as she knew, Anthony still lived in New Jersey. No way he'd see them together on the subway later.

"Yeah, I came in earlier than usual to catch up on work and ran into Kate on her walk to," Jon said, smooth as silk.

And why wouldn't his answer sound natural? Jon had run into her on her walk to work, albeit the meet was intentional on his part.

Jon and Anthony followed her into the building and across the lobby to the elevator. Both men waited for Kate to step in first, which was polite, but grated on her some. Jon almost made her laugh when he positioned himself at an angle between her and Anthony, almost like a protective shield. When the corners of Anthony's mouth turned up, she resisted touching her fingers to her cheek to see whether the warmth of Jon's nearness was obvious.

The elevator stopped at their floor.

Anthony held the door open. "Jon, I need you to clarify some information on the work you did for me. Stop by my cubicle before you get into whatever you're working on for Kate."

Jon visibly stiffened. The tone of Anthony's request was more on the order of a command.

"I have a few minutes I can spare," Jon said.

Kate sighed with relief when she parted ways with the two men and the testosterone charged atmosphere surrounding them. She had a bad feeling that keeping her work and her fledgling relationship completely compartmentalized was going to be more difficult than she'd thought. Her mind swirled with conflicting thoughts. Wasn't that the premise of the No Brides vow? Career and romantic relationships were mutually exclusive. Her chest tightened. But her heart screamed something altogether different.

JON CLENCHED and unclenched his hands over his laptop as he caught the motion of Kate leaving for the day, right on time as they'd planned. He could have decked Anthony this morning if he were that type of man, which he wasn't. Or hadn't been until Kate had agreed to give a relationship a try. After the smirky looks Anthony had given Kate this morning, the guy's inuendo about thawing the ice queen had almost made Jon lose it. But he'd controlled himself. Losing his temper with Anthony would have been shouting that he and Kate had something going on. So he'd answered Anthony's asinine work questions as professionally as he could, gotten back to his cubicle, and dived into his work for Kate. The busier he was, the faster the day would go. But it still hadn't gone fast enough.

Twenty minutes of clock-watching later, Jon shut his computer down and left the office and his unfinished spreadsheet behind. It could wait until Monday. His mind wasn't in it. He'd done the last calculation twice and still wasn't sure he'd used the right assumptions. Jon wove his way around other, slower-walking pedestrians on the sidewalk to the Chamber Street station, getting to the turnstiles well ahead of their meeting time. He swiped his MTA card, walked through, and glanced toward the platform. No Kate, but he hadn't expected her yet. Jon paced back and forth where he was. Catching her at the turnstiles struck him as a better idea than possibly missing her on the platform and having to connect with her at Penn Station.

Jon stopped mid-pace. He hadn't factored in time for Kate to get an MTA card. He blew out a breath. She lived in New York. She'd have one. He started and stopped his pacing. But—he slapped the side of his head with his palm —he hadn't thought about her needing an Amtrak ticket. He hadn't even told Kate which Amtrak train he took, so she'd know if they didn't connect at the subway station. Jon shook his head in disgust. He hadn't been this twisted with uncertainty since he'd left his parents' house for college.

A tap on his shoulder made him jump.

"You just get here, too?" Kate asked.

He blinked at her. "You have an MTA card."

"Ye-ah. Why?"

"Never mind." He didn't need to tell Kate what a buffoon he was. She'd find out soon enough if he didn't get himself together.

The sound of an approaching subway train echoed through the tunnel. "We'd better get over to the platform,"

Jon moved his hand to take Kate's overnight bag, but a glance from her stopped him. Manners drilled into him as a kid versus Kate's independence. They poured into the open train door with the rest of the crowd. The train took off.

"Right on schedule," Kate said over her shoulder, said shoulder touching his chest, closing the minute space between them.

"Yep," he said noticing the fresh flowery scent of her hair. No, he would have noticed that at work. She must have put on perfume. For him? He cleared his throat. "When we get to Penn, you should have just enough time to get your Amtrak ticket."

"Not to worry. I got an eTicket before I left the office."

As he would have, but he hadn't told her which train.

"The Empire service to Albany, leaving at 5:47," she said.

He grasped the strap tighter and locked his knees to counter the relief flowing through him that he hadn't let whatever idiocy that had taken hold of him blurt out his concerns about MTA cards or train tickets.

The subway train became more crowded with every stop, making conversation difficult and keeping Kate pressed against him and the temperature in the car rising. By the time they'd transferred to Amtrak at Penn Station and found seats together, Jon felt like he'd just finished a record-setting 1,500-meter freestyle swim race.

"You do this every day," Kate said, stowing her bag by her feet. "Makes me appreciate my walk to work."

"It's not so bad, and the trade off is that I get to live in Columbia County."

"It is beautiful there, reminds me of Genesee, except you have the rolling hills of the river valley and mountains nearby, not just flat fields."

Jon's ears perked up. Had he caught a wistful edge to Kate's voice? Could she give up the city life—except for work? He reined in his enthusiasm. That consideration was a ways off, a long ways off. He and Kate hadn't even been on a real date together, unless he counted dinner with his grandfather after the swim meet. On the other hand, he'd been on countless dates with countless women and never considered bringing them to the farm, let alone thought about them living there. He frowned. Except Olivia, and she'd thrown him over for a doctor with a fancier house in the Westchester suburbs closer to New York.

"What?" Kate asked, looking from side to side. "You look like you just got a whiff of something rotten."

"A rotten thought." He grabbed the first one besides Olivia and her betrayal that came to mind. "Anthony."

Kate laughed. "I can't disagree. "Something in particular?"

"Something he said to me this morning when we were going over the questions he had about my report. Garbage, really, but it made me think that we should watch how we act with each other at work."

Kate nodded. "I was going to talk to you about that."

Was this where she gave him a walk back to just being friends?

"Kim saw us at the Briarwood."

"I know. I was there when she came over to talk with you."

"The kiss."

"Oh, that."

"Yes, that," Kate almost huffed.

"Nice," he decreed, weighing what she would do if he repeated it here.

Kate's eyes darkened before she gave him a playful slug. "Be serious."

"I was."

She rolled her eyes. "Anyway, Kim cautioned us to be discreet while you're working as my assistant. The boss-subordinate thing."

"I agree. It shouldn't be problem at work."

"Right. We'll just have to watch ourselves at places like the Briarwood, where we might run into someone from DeBakker."

He could watch Kate anytime. The way she crinkled her nose when she was thinking hard, bit her bottom lip when she was deciding how to word something, smoothed her hair when she was nervous.

The ping of her cell phone interrupted his pleasant thoughts.

"I should check that." She pulled out her phone, looked at the screen, and looped her hair behind her ear. "The mortgage broker," she said before she touched the text icon.

Jon saw her eyes widen. *Yep*, watch her anytime, all the time, and never be bored.

"Yes!" Kate fist pumped, phone in hand. She grabbed his

arm with her other hand and squeezed. "I've been pre-approved for the mortgage on the apartment."

"Congratulations!"

When she released his arm and he slid it across the back of her seat and squeezed her shoulder. "We have more to celebrate this weekend."

Kate grinned and let him keep his arm around her.

Jon relaxed back in his seat and allowed the rhythm of the train to lull him. He shouldn't have let Anthony's actions and words this morning get to him and clutter his mind with garbage.

He glanced at Kate texting the broker back. It was going to be a great weekend.

The June sunlight through the kitchen window was almost blinding. No hint of the possible rain showers in the morning that had been forecast yesterday. Jon took a carton of eggs and a package of bacon out of the refrigerator. He'd been up at the crack of dawn, moved the cattle to today's grazing area, and checked his email, both work and personal, and still no sounds of anyone else being awake. A door opened and closed in the hallway, followed by another door opening and closing.

Someone was up. Jon reached into the cupboard for a mixing bowl, but waited on the scrambled eggs and bacon he'd been about to start. Maybe Kate didn't like bacon and eggs. His grandfather had made her pancakes. He sipped his coffee.

"Hi." Kate stood in the kitchen doorway, dressed in jeans and a light blue t-shirt with some kind of lacy stuff around the front neckline. Her hair was down, loose around her shoulders, the way he liked it best.

"Good morning. I was about to make scrambled eggs and bacon. That is if you like scrambled eggs." He held his breath as if it really mattered whether she liked scrambled eggs or not and quickly released it when he felt stupid—not a feeling he was accustomed to, except when he was around Kate. "We have English muffins and bread for toast, too."

"Scrambled eggs and bacon sound great. I'll grab a cup of coffee."

He stood still as she moved to squeeze between him and the table, remembering his somewhat tortuous subway ride with Kate so close in front of him. Once she'd passed by, Jon began cracking eggs into the bowl.

"Can you hand me the half and half?" he asked when she finished fixing her coffee. Their fingers touched, shooting a tingle up his arm. In reaction, he grasped the carton until it began to crush in his hand. "If you want toast or a muffin, they're in the bread box next to the coffee maker."

He relaxed as she moved a couple feet away from him and opened the bread box. Jon poured some half and half in the bowl and whipped the eggs harder than necessary with the fork. He had to man-up and stop reverting to his teenage self every time Kate got closer than a foot away from him.

"What's going on here?" his grandfather's voice boomed from the doorway.

Jon tensed. Grandpa couldn't have been reading his mind, could he? Jon wouldn't put anything past the old guy. He followed his grandfather's gaze to Kate putting a muffin in the toaster next to the bread box.

"You're our guest, Kate. Jon shouldn't be putting you to work."

Jon relaxed, stopped beating the eggs, and poured the mixture into the frying pan.

"It's no problem," Kate said.

Jon opened the bacon and turned on the stovetop griddle.

His grandfather walked over. "You should put that bacon in the broiler. Dottie said it crisps up nicer and the excess fat drains off."

Jon bit back a smile, opened the broiler door of the stove and pulled out the broiler pan. "Well, if Dottie says so." He began laying the bacon out on the pan.

His grandfather crossed the room to the coffee maker. "Good thing you were up early. We're going to have to leave at 7:50, instead of eight."

"Why's that?" Jon asked.

"We have to swing by and pick up Dottie. She wants to see the parade, and she couldn't talk anyone in her family into going. No sense in her driving to Hudson by herself. I offered to take her."

His grandfather turned toward the coffeemaker to pour a cup and Jon caught Kate's gaze over the older man's bent head. "So like a double date," Jon said.

She grinned. He grinned back, warmed that he and Kate were on the same wavelength.

"No," his grandfather sputtered. "Like being neighborly. Shouldn't you be getting that bacon in the broiler?"

"On it," Jon said, while Kate covered her mouth with her hand. She couldn't disguise the laughter in her eyes, though.

Two hours later, the four of them were seated in lawn chairs beside the street in Hudson near the end of the parade route. Jon had set his and Kate's chairs up with the arms touching, so that when they sat, her right arm rested against his.

"The parade's coming." Kate scooted forward in her chair and looked up the street. "I can hear the music."

Jon strained his ears and followed her gaze up the empty street.

"There." She pointed.

Jon slid his arm over onto the edge of her chair's armrest, palm up.

"See."

Jon spotted the colors of the parade's front banner. "I do now."

Kate grabbed for the front edge of the arm rest to slide back in her chair and he curled his fingers through hers.

She squeezed his hand. *Mission accomplished.*

The parade was in full view, coming up on them quickly. The local volunteer fire departments, high school bands, drum and bugle corps, veterans, little league ballplayers, girl and boy scouts, and local politicos marched by.

"Listen," Kate said. "There's a bagpipe band coming. I love the sound of bagpipes. I've thought of learning how to play, like I have enough free time for lessons and practicing. Maybe someday." Her voice trailed off.

If only he could show Kate she could have a lot more in her life than work. Of course, it had taken almost losing is grandfather for him to see that.

"Know what this reminds me of?" she asked.

"No, tell me."

"The Fire Department Parade and Carnival in Genesee." Kate turned to Jon's grandfather and Dottie. "There are two parades, actually. The first night to open the carnival, there's one like this one with volunteer fire companies from all over Western New York. The other is the second night with floats made by organizations and kids' groups that are judged. Awards are given out at a ceremony afterwards. And there's carnival rides and games for all ages." She glanced over at Jon. "You remember."

She didn't wait for an answer, but dove back into her explanation for his grandfather and Dottie. "One year, when my brother and I were crazy about dinosaurs and cavemen, we got some friends together, pooled all our money for the entry fee, and made a caveman float. We got second place for our age group." She ended with a flourish.

Watching Kates's gestures and enthusiasm took the sting out of his non-answer to her *you remember*. He didn't remember. He'd never been. When he was young, things like that were too crowded, noisy, and dirty for his parents. Besides, they were probably working. He couldn't remember anyone ever inviting him as a teen.

"I hope you're not disappointed by our Flag Day celebration," his grandfather said. "We don't have much in the way of rides and carnival games."

"But there's all kinds of food and crafts, and local businesses and organizations have booths. Not to mention a picturesque walking path along the riverfront, and if you want to stay that late, fireworks over the river at dusk. They put on a great show." Jon snapped his mouth shut. He'd sounded like a cross between the celebration's PR committee and a ten-year-old boy focused on food and fireworks.

"I'm sure I'll enjoy myself. Half the fun of these things is the people you're with, and I can't imagine a better group." She squeezed his hand.

He took the squeeze as a sign that she didn't think he was a babbling idiot. If he'd relax and let himself, he expected he'd have a good time, too. Beautiful day. A beautiful woman with him. No work pressures or demands or worries about his and Kate's coworkers seeing them together, not having to hide his feelings in front of others. Today was just what he and Kate needed.

～

KATE HAD BEEN SO comfortable sitting hand in hand with Jon that she hated to get up after the last of the parade passed by them. Living in the city for so long, she'd almost forgotten some of the simple small-town things she'd liked about Genesee. In a way, Jon had the best of both worlds here. He could easily get to things in the city and have the relaxing bucolic atmosphere of rural living when he was home. Although the train ride getting up here yesterday had seemed long, she could almost see herself making the commute. She shook the thought from her head. What was she thinking? She was about to buy her Tribeca apartment.

"If you're not ready for lunch then ..." Jon started.

"What?"

"I asked if you wanted to get lunch or walk around some first and you shook your head."

"I was lost in thought. Why don't we look around first, see what's here, what booths we want to check out after lunch?"

"Sounds like a plan."

Jon rose and tugged Kate to her feet with his still entwined hand. He was so close. She raised her head. Close enough to kiss her. And unlike at the Briarwood, there wasn't anyone from work to see them. She leaned closer as if drawn by a magnetic force. Jon bent his head.

"Dottie and I are going to catch up with the guys at the VFW booth," his grandfather said.

Kate and Jon jumped apart. No co-workers, but there *was* Pete.

"You can take our chairs back to the car with yours, and we'll connect with you later."

"Copy that," Jon said.

When Pete and Dottie were out of hearing range, Kate asked, "Did he do that on purpose?"

"Probably." Jon leaned over and gave her a lingering peck on the lips before gathering and folding the four chairs. Just as the zing of his surprise kiss was winding down, he wrapped his free hand around hers sending her nerve endings back into overdrive.

A warm flood of contentment, infused her. If she didn't watch it, she'd be purring like a cat.

As if her musing was a trigger, the first booth they approached was the Columbia-Greene Humane Society's.

"Look, kittens!" Kate tugged Jon toward the Society's tables of cages. "Let's look at them first, before we do our walk around to see what else is here."

"Sure." The corners of his mouth curved up.

"It's an adoption clinic," she said. Stopping in front of the cages with cats, Kate realized she still held Jon's hand. She loosened her grip and he tightened his. *Okay.* She left her hand where it was and smiled over her shoulder at Jon, catching him inches away, studying her. Kate cleared her dry throat. "Do you and Pete have a cat? I didn't notice when I was at the house."

"We did." Jon similarly cleared his throat and her heart skipped a beat.

Either there was something going around causing dry throats, or their closeness was affecting Jon like it was affecting her.

"Our cat died a few months ago," he said. She was Grandma's, lived to be 17."

"Living in the country, we always had a cat or two to keep the house mouse-free when I was growing up." Kate stuck her finger in the cage and waited for one of the kittens to come over so she could pet its nose. "They're so cute. You should get one."

"What about you?"

Jon's breath ticked her ear, making her shiver despite the warm summer air.

"You said your building allows pets"

Kate looked at the kittens wistfully.

"Hi, are you interested in a kitten?"

Kate pulled her gaze from the now-wrestling kittens and focused on the woman with a volunteer badge standing on the other side of the table. "They *are* adorable. But they're babies. I wouldn't feel right leaving one home alone all day while I work." She looked back at Jon as if needing him to justify her not giving in to her longing to take one of the kittens. "You know my hours,"

Instead of backing her up, he reached around her and wiggled his finger in the cage. One of the kittens tried to pounce on it. "I don't know. This guy is pretty brave. He might be okay on his own during the day."

She shot him a *thanks a lot* look, as her opposition began to crumble.

"How about an older cat? We have several." The volunteer moved down the table to a pair of cages.

"Check them out. You know you want to." Jon stepped back so she could move down the table without bumping into him.

Even though he was exasperating her with his prodding, she had to admit she did want to check out the cats. It would be nice to have something to come home to. But not as nice as having some*one* to come home to. Her stomach flip-flopped at her next thought of that someone being Jon, of coming home to him and one of the kittens, or a pair of kittens.

She moved down the table to clear her mind before she did anything she'd regret later.

The volunteer held an orange tiger cat in her arms. "This sweetie is one of a sister pair whose owner had to give them up when she was transferred to the UK for work." She lifted the cat toward Kate. "Want to hold her?"

Of course, she did. But would she want to hand her back?

"Go for it." Jon said.

She did, reaching forward if only to put some distance between her and Jon, who stood uncomfortably close behind her again. Uncomfortably in a good way. A way that lifted her heart and made her want to smile, in addition to heightening all of her senses.

"This girl's name is Scarlet. She and her sister are used to being alone during the work day," the volunteer said.

The cat cuddled into her arms and she nuzzled the animal's soft fur.

Jon reached over her shoulder to pet the cat, too. His finger grazed Kate's cheek, the roughness of his working man hands contrasting with the cat's soft fur.

"Would you like to hold her sister Crimson?" The volunteer lifted an identical cat from the cage.

"You know you do," Kate teased.

Jon reached over and lifted the cat from the volunteer, putting some breathing room between the two of them. "So, Scarlet and Crimson?"

"That's right. If possible, we'd like to keep the two cats together." The volunteer glanced from Kate and the cat she held to Jon and the cat in his arms, a glint of question in her gaze.

"Oh, we're not together," Kate stuttered. "I mean we don't live together." Her mind flew back to her earlier thought of coming home to Jon before darting to wondering why she'd blurted their living arrangements. "We ..." Where was that invisible support she'd felt from Jon before?

He chuckled, stopping her mental stumble, redirecting it to irritation.

"I think if we each adopted one of these beauties, we could manage to get them together regularly."

Kate's irritation melted away. Jon spoke as if they were already a done deal, not just exploring whether they'd work as a couple. While as an independent career woman, she should object to Jon moving them forward like that, somehow she didn't.

"We won't be leaving for quite awhile," Jon said, "so we can't take them now."

"You each need to fill out an application first, anyway, and we need to review them," the volunteer said.

Jon and Kate handed the cats back, filled out the pet adoption applications and gave them to the volunteer.

"Be sure to stop back before five," she said. "We'll be starting to take everything down then."

Kate spent the afternoon pleasantly on pins and needles that she wanted to attribute to the anticipation of her new pet, but more likely was due to Jon keeping her hand firmly in his or his arm protectively around her shoulders as they visited every booth at the celebration. At 4:45, they headed back to the Humane Society booth.

"Here you are," the volunteer greeted them. "Everything is set. I just need you to sign our pet adoption agreement and make your donation. Take a minute to read it."

Kate skimmed down the paper and signed at the bottom. She dug in her purse for her checkbook, looking up to see Jon hand over his credit card.

"For both."

When Kate opened her mouth to protest, Jon placed his index finger over her lips. He took his time removing it, stilling her outside and inciting turmoil inside.

"You can cover dinner," he said.

That warmed her almost as much as his touch had.

The volunteer took their agreements and Jon's card and returned with two cat carriers.

Kate leaned over and peeked in the carriers. She straightened and smiled. Before she could tell him they'd have to do takeout for dinner because they couldn't leave the cats in the car, Jon lowered his head and pressed his lips to hers. Everything but Jon's touch, his solidness to her softness, zapped from her mind, as if there was nothing in the world but him, the warm sunshine on them and the fire inside her.

After he'd broken the kiss and she'd recovered her ability to breathe, she asked "What was that for?"

"Because I wanted to." Jon lifted one of the cat carriers.

Still dazed, Kate reached for the other cat carrier and a caught a motion out of the corner of her eye. A man staring at them. A man that her quick glance said was familiar, but who turned before she could identify him.

Her stomach knotted in a fear she couldn't identify.

JON COULDN'T TELL if he was relieved or irritated that his grandfather and Dottie caught up with him and Kate as they were leaving the Humane Society booth. Their kiss had rocked him to his foundation and added fuel to the argument that he was falling for Kate—hard. Falling in a way far beyond the torch he carried for her in high school. Beyond anything he'd experienced as an adult. But the way Kate had gone from the woman who'd seemed to melt into his kiss to the tense distant person walking beside him had rocked him, too, and not in a good way. He wanted to talk with her privately, but feared what she might say,

"What have you got there?" his grandfather asked.

"Cats," Kate said with strained cheerfulness. Or his old-time insecurities were surfacing to make it sound strained to him.

"Sisters. One for your house and one for me," she continued.

"Scarlet and Crimson," Jon added.

"Let me see," Dottie said.

Jon lifted his carrier to her eye level.

"Pretty animal."

"Kate's cat looks just like her," he said. "Hope you don't mind if we skip staying for the fireworks. I'm not sure how the cats would be."

"Fine with me," his grandfather said.

"Me, too." A chime from Dottie's cell phone interrupted the conversation. She pulled her phone out of her bag and frowned. "It's a text from Gavin, says urgent." She tapped the screen and her eyes grew wide. "We need to leave now. He heard on his scanner that the fire department was called to your place."

"The barn?" Jon asked. He'd talked to Grandpa and Gavin about leaving rags with linseed oil on them in the barn.

"It doesn't say. Should I call him?" Dottie asked.

"No, we'd better just go. You can call him in the car."

Kate reached over and squeezed the top of his closest hand, the hand holding the cat carrier, dissolving part of the lump in his throat.

Jon made it back to the farm in record time. The volunteer fire company's fire chief's pickup and two fire trucks were there. He couldn't see any flames, although from what he could tell, firefighters were still spraying water on the back of the house.

The chief walked over to Jon's car as he got out. "We have the fire out. We're just dousing some hot spots. A kitchen fire, maybe electric."

Jon had been after his grandfather to have the house wiring updated. He sighed. He should have made arrangements himself. But the house was Grandpa's. Jon only had an interest in the barn and cattle operation.

"We limited the fire damage to the kitchen. There's smoke and water damage. Any pets besides the dog?"

"No just Barney," who brushed against his leg as Jon was talking.

The chief nodded. "We'll finish up and come back tomorrow when we have better light to determine the cause for sure and give you a report for your insurer. You'll need to stay somewhere else for a couple days, board off the kitchen until you can have it repaired.

"Will we be able to go in the house tomorrow for clothes and things?"

"You should be okay."

Thanks." Jon looked to where his grandfather stood near the side of the house. He was staring at the back. *Insurance* flashed in Jon's head like a neon sign. He knew there was a farm policy on the barn, farm equipment, and cattle. The bank had required it for the home equity loan, and he'd bought it himself. His grandfather *must* have homeowner's insurance, too, or he wouldn't have gotten the loan. But Jon couldn't remember paying any premiums since he'd been overseeing his grandfather's finances.

He sensed Kate next to him before he saw her.

She touched his arm. "You okay?"

"Yeah." Somehow, her being there made him okay, even if he really wasn't. "I don't know about Grandpa, though."

"Go to him."

"Amy's kitchen," he heard his grandfather repeating as he approached him.

"Grandpa."

His grandfather looked at him, his eyes watery. "After your mother finished college, I remodeled the kitchen myself." His voice cracked. "Just like your grandmother had always wanted."

"It's okay, Grandpa. We'll redo it." He put his arm around the older man's shoulders and nudged him away from the house. They took a couple steps, and his grandfather stumbled. As if appearing out of nowhere, Kate was on his grandfather's other side to help Jon catch him.

"Are you all right?" Jon asked.

"Yep," his grandfather said. "Bum leg. Tripped on a rock," he muttered.

Dottie joined them. "I talked with the chief. You all can come and stay at my house as long as you need to. I've got plenty of room."

"Thanks," Jon said. "The chief said we should be able to get into the house for clothes and stuff tomorrow. Go back to the car, and I'll tell the chief we're leaving." Barney nudged his hand and whimpered.

"Barney can come, too," Dottie said. "I have the old dog run I'm not using that opens into the garage for shelter. Some dog food, too, in the garage, left over from Shep. The cats can come in the house."

"Thanks." Jon felt like he'd said that 100 times in the last ten minutes.

At Dottie's, Jon got Barney settled while the others went

into the house. Kate met him on the wraparound front porch.

"Dottie's making tea," Kate said

"Of course she is." It was good to have something ordinary happening. "She makes tea for any and all occasions."

Kate stepped forward and wrapped her arms around him, laying her head on his chest. He could feel her heart beating with his. "What's that for?" he asked into her hair.

"Because I wanted to," she repeated his answer to his kiss earlier today, what seemed like a lifetime ago.

Her hug was what he needed, wanted, too. For the moment, the fire, all his responsibilities, the list of things he'd have to do disappeared. There was only the woman he loved—*yes*, he loved her—holding him under the dusky summer sky and his heart hoping that she just might love him, too.

$\mathcal{K}$ate tried to blame her inability to fall asleep and stay asleep on Jon and his grandfather's misfortune and staying in a strange place. But she knew that those factors were a small part of her insomnia. The real problem was that in defiance of her No Brides vow and her recent determination to keep her relationship with Jon in the friends arena until she had her promotion to fund manager, she was falling for him. Apparently, her heart was with a different program and no matter how hard she tried to push down her feeling and argue logic with them, she couldn't do it 100%.

She rolled over and pulled the covers over her head as if that would do anything. A knock at the door startled her upright. Jon? She wrapped her covers around herself.

"Kate, are you awake?" Dottie's voice came through the door. It's eight. Jon and my grandson Gavin went over to do morning chores a while ago and should be back soon to take you to collect your things."

"I'm up. I'll be out in a minute." *Or so.* She rarely slept until eight, even on weekends. The rise and shine farm time ingrained in her from childhood wouldn't let her. Kate smoothed the t-shirt from yesterday that she'd slept in and pulled on her jeans, running her tongue around her mouth. A quick shower and mouth rinse were in order. She glanced in the mirror. And her hair. She had a comb in her purse and could braid it back, although she suspected Jon preferred it down.

Kate walked into Dottie's kitchen feeling somewhat cleaner and groomed as Jon and Dottie's grandson came in the outside door. Jon was as disheveled looking as she'd felt. He'd replaced his polo shirt from yesterday with a plain white t-shirt that had a smudge across the front where he must have leaned against equipment or something or wiped mud off his hand. His well-worn jeans had a hole in one knee and hung low on his slim hips. On him, disheveled looked sexy.

"We have the okay from the fire company to go into the house, other than the kitchen," Jon said. "Grandpa, I'll take you and Kate over when you two are ready."

"You and Kate go ahead," Pete said. "Dottie will take me over later, after church. Did you bring me some clean clothes?"

Jon lifted the canvas travel bag he had in his hand. "I'll clean up while Kate has her breakfast and leave the bag in the bathroom for you."

Kate watched him disappear through the doorway, noticing a slight slump to his broad shoulders.

Fifteen minutes later, they were headed for the farmhouse.

"How does the house look?" she asked when the silence in the car threatened to suffocate her.

"Most of the downstairs has smoke damage. Some water damage in the dining room. The upstairs not so much. I opened windows in the living room, dining room, and the bedrooms, downstairs and upstairs. The breeze today will help. I'll contact a fire cleanup and restoration outfit tomorrow. The kitchen is a total loss."

"And?" Kate sensed there was more.

Jon took so long to answer that she thought he wasn't going to.

"I dug out Grandpa's homeowner's insurance policy last night. He doesn't have full value replacement coverage and has a high deductible. You heard Grandpa say, the kitchen was last updated more than 35 years ago. The insurance isn't going to cover much."

A muscle worked in Jon's jaw, and Kate waited for him to continue.

He cleared his throat. "When I left the private equity firm, I ploughed most of my free cash into our beef operation. It wasn't the wisest move I've ever made," he added in a voice barely above a whisper.

Kate's chest tightened. *He was embarrassed.*

"I know most farms, especially start-ups operate on a thin margin," she said, warmed that he was sharing this with her.

"I have investments I could liquidate, but you know where the market is right now. I'd have to take a loss." His voice took on a defensive tone.

Kate touched his arm to assure him she wasn't making any judgments.

"Grandpa has a home equity loan on the property that he took out to pay for the new barn. A loan he can barely afford on his income. That's why I took the job offer from DeBakker for the summer. To get ahead, possibly pay off, his loan and give Grandpa a financial cushion. Now that summer income will have to go toward repairing the house." Jon lifted his hand from the steering wheel and ran it through his hair. "I don't know why I'm dumping all this on you."

"I do," she said. "Because you need to get it out and figured I'd understand. That I care." She held her breath while she waited for his reaction to her words.

He placed his hand on her knee. "Yes," he said simply. Jon put his hand back on the steering wheel. "And I care about you, too. A lot."

Kate's heart thumped against her chest.

"This all has a point," Jon said in a controlled voice.

Her heart stilled. Obviously, a point other than them admitting feelings for each other.

"Does DeBakker farm out any of its back-office work to remote employees?" he asked.

Work. Of course, work. She was the person who'd made a vow to put work first. Why shouldn't she expect Jon to do the same. *Because I want more than just work success now.* She answered her own question.

"If so, I was thinking of checking with HR about staying on, handling back office overflow when needed from my home office in addition to teaching. Maybe that would get management off my back about taking one of the portfolio manager openings."

"There are two manager positions now." Her thoughts drifted to the scenario she'd pictured the other day of him staying at DeBakker and each of them managing a fund.

"If you're testing whether I'm competition for your promotion, the answer is no."

"N-no," she stammered. She wasn't secure enough in her feelings or his feelings to share her daydream, or even if she'd want to have a long-term relationship with someone she worked with every day. Her stomach knotted. How had she gotten them into a long-term relationship?

"Teaching and managing the farm is what I want to be doing." Jon said.

"DeBakker does use remote employees for some of its back-office work." Kate brought herself back to safer territory.

"Hmm?" Jon said.

Were his thoughts somewhere else, too? "The back-office work you asked about."

"Right. I'll check with HR tomorrow. But I'm looking at the back-office work, if it's even an option in August when my statistician gig is up, as temporary until the farm business is back on its feet."

Kate's imagination flitted ahead. Where would she and Jon be if they didn't have the DeBakker connection? *Focus*, she admonished herself. Her primary focus should be on getting her promotion. But the closer she and Jon got, the harder it was to maintain that focus.

HE AND KATE didn't spend much time in the farmhouse getting her things and more clothes for him, but as he started the drive back to Dottie's with her, the stench of burned wood still seemed to fill his nostrils. Jon turned on the AC to clear the air, hopefully in more ways than one. Since they'd arrived at the farmhouse, Kate had distanced herself. Right now she was silently typing into her phone. He couldn't figure out if it was because he and she had admitted feelings for each other, that she didn't believe him and thought he still wanted one of the portfolio manager positions, or that she did believe him and his lack of ambition for the big bucks diminished him in her eyes.

It was his own fault for spilling his personal financial situation instead of simply asking her what she knew about DeBakker's back office personnel hiring practices. But then they wouldn't have admitted their feelings, which was good. Wasn't it?

Kate made a grumbly sound and frowned at her phone. "I can't find out whether I can take Scarlet with me on the train home. One place it says *yes*. Another it says *no*. In a third, it says *on certain trains*. Then, it doesn't say which ones."

"I didn't consider that yesterday," he said.

"Me either."

"I know." His spirits lifted at the thought. "I'll drive you and Scarlet home. If I can use your parking privileges at your apartment building, it would be easier for me to stay in the city for a couple days until Grandpa and I can get back in the farmhouse. Not impose on Dottie, wake her up when I have to get up at the crack of dawn to make my train," It also might give him a couple evenings with Kate after work.

"But the expense of a hotel."

Jon cringed. "I didn't mean to make my situation sound dire. It was more musing, thinking long term, and beating myself up some for not checking Grandpa's homeowner's insurance more closely when I took over managing his finances. He pays it annually, so it didn't pop up on my radar when I was paying his other bills."

"You don't need to explain."

Of course he didn't. He was just running on again about something of no interest to Kate.

She looked pensive. "Maybe I should take both cats until you and your grandfather are settled back in your house and the kitchen area is partitioned off."

"Trying to steal my cat?"

"No. But cats can be strange about being moved to a new place. You don't want her to get out when the restoration or remodeling people are going in and out and take off somewhere."

Jon released the laugh he'd been holding in, and it felt good. "I was kidding."

"Oh."

"But that's a good idea. We'll stop at the grocery store for whatever pet supplies you'll need on our way. Want to get going as soon as we get back to Dottie's and corral the cats?"

"I want to change first, but yeah."

"Great. While you do that, I'll make some calls to line up a place in the city to stay for a few days."

Kate bit her lower lip and released it as if she was going to say something, but she didn't.

This time he was able to keep his mouth shut and drive, even though he wanted to ask what she was thinking.

A few minutes later, they were back at Dottie's. Jon handed Kate her overnight bag from the back of the car, leaving his gym bag and the two suit bags with his work clothes where they were. They headed in the front door to the living room.

"I'll wait here," Jon said, sliding his phone out of his pocket. He waited until she'd turned and started up the stairs to start his calls.

"It wasn't me. Promise."

Kate's words spoken numerous-calls-to-hotels later pulled Jon's attention from his phone.

"What?"

"Your expression," Kate said. "You look like you're ready to tear something apart."

He rose from the couch as she walked into the living

room wearing a pair of navy pants that ended at her shapely calves—he never remembered what those pants were called—and a nautical stripped shirt. Her hair was pulled back into a pony tail that swung with her steps. He ran his hand through his hair. When he'd cleaned up, he'd just traded his white t-shirt and old jeans for a colored t-shirt and an equally worn pair of jeans sans the hole in the knee.

Jon clicked his phone screen off. "I hadn't realized how hard it would be to book somewhere to stay on such short notice. I've tried everywhere I've stayed before and couldn't get a room at any of them."

Kate looked toward the doorway to the dining room and kitchen, as if making sure they were alone, and then back at him. "I have a pullout loveseat. You could stay at my apartment for a couple of days."

"Kate, Kate." Someone gently shook her shoulder, and she jerked awake. She was in the car, Jon's car."

He smiled over at her. "You fell asleep about 30 miles into the drive."

She looked out the windshield. They were close to Murray Street.

"I need directions to the entrance to your building's parking garage."

"Right."

"Here?" Jon flipped on the car's directional.

"No." Kate shook her head as if that would clear her mind, which was filled with remnants of vague dreams in which Jon had played a major role. "Two blocks up, at the light."

"You okay?" he asked, concern coming through in his voice.

"Yes, sill waking up."

Jon turned at the light.

"Now right again into the garage. The way I almost immediately doze off, I'm probably not your—anyone's—first choice as a driving companion.

Jon mumbled something that sounded like "I don't know about that." But that could have been her brain fog talking.

"Third level," she said once they were in the garage.

Jon parked and went around to the back of the vehicle to open the hatch, while Kate got the cat carriers out of the back seat. By the time she joined him, he had his suit bags and was lifting out her overnight case.

"I'll take that if you can take one of the cats." She placed Crimson's crate just inside the cargo area and reached for the overnight bag, watching the play in his forearm muscle as he handed it to her. "I feel better if we're one-on-one with the cats."

"Where to?" he asked.,

"The elevators." She pointed to the back wall of the garage. "With my swiper key, we can take one up to my floor."

"Lead the way," he said.

Rather than follow, Jon matched her step for step, his left arm with the suit bags slung over it brushing her arm almost every step. What had she been thinking, inviting him to stay in her place, her small, barely more than an efficiency apartment, place.

As they approached the bay of elevators, her next-door neighbor called from an open, crowded one, "Want me to hold it?"

She waved him off. "No, go ahead, we'll take the next one." An elevator that only had her and Jon would be too small a space for the both of them. Jon's nearness on the crowded one might be the breaking point of her mishmash of feeling.

Kate pulled her key card out of her pants pocket where she'd put it before she'd gotten out of the car. She inserted and withdrew it from the slot in the center of the bank of elevators.

"After you," Jon said.

She stepped in and moved to the far left to press the button for the third floor. Jon went to the left, keeping his armful of suit bags between them, a well-measured distance away. Maybe Jon's insides were as jumbled as hers. Somehow, she liked that thought.

"My apartment is this way," she said as they left the elevator on the third floor.

"I know," he said.

There was no logical reason him remembering which direction her apartment was would be something that should affect her heart rate, but it had. She stopped at her door. "Here we are." Kate's voice sounded gravelly to her.

Jon just smiled. Was he enjoying putting her off-kilter? She opened the door locks. Or was it all in her mind? Maybe Jon's stay would just be for tonight. She eyed his two suit bags. That didn't look like what he was planning.

Kate pushed the door open. "You can put your suits in the closet next to the door and other things in the bathroom."

"Okay, and thanks again." Jon's phone pinged. "The Greenwich." He read the text. "They have a room for tomorrow and Tuesday night."

"If you want. But you're free to stay here." The words

came out as if her mouth wasn't connected to her brain. A minute ago, she was hoping he'd only be here one night.

Indecision clouded Jon's handsome features. His eyes darkened. "I'd just as soon be ... stay with you. If you're sure."

"I'm sure." She couldn't take back her invitation now. Nor did she want to. What could be a better way to test their compatibility, prove or disprove Kate's concern about having a relationship with someone she also worked with than a few days together 24/7?

Jon's smile went straight to her heart. "I'll just put my stuff away. In my room." She pointed at the doorway and made her escape.

After centering herself as best she could, Kate rejoined Jon a couple of minutes later. He'd let Scarlet and Crimson out and the felines were making themselves at home on the back of her loveseat. "I hope you don't mind pizza for Sunday dinner. I just ordered one, along with wings."

"Good with me, as long as I don't have to chase the delivery person down again. I'm still getting the kinks out of my legs from the drive and the fact that I haven't made swim practices for nearly a week."

"Nope, no delivery person chasing is on the agenda for today. If you want, though, you can go down to the Equinox and swim or workout. I can call the pizzeria back and have them hold off on the pizza delivery for an hour."

"That sounds great. I'll get my workout stuff and head down."

"And I'll get the cats' stuff set up. Kate dropped to the couch as soon as the apartment door closed behind Jon.

If she was this much of a mess after having Jon in her apartment for 15 minutes, what would she be like after a couple of days?

THE SWIM WAS JUST what Jon needed to get rid of the nervous energy that had been building in him since he'd pulled his car into the parking garage of Kate's building. He might still be able to grab that reservation at the Greenwich Hotel. But he didn't want to. Bunking at her place for a couple of nights would let him get to know Kate better, uncensored by work constraints. He zipped his bag. He couldn't remember wanting to do that with any woman in a long time. Or maybe ever.

A familiar-sounding voice interrupted his thoughts. Someone from DeBakker, though he couldn't put a face to the voice. He ducked behind a nearby pillar in the gym locker room until the voice drifted away, out the door. He'd better take the stairs up instead of the elevator, and he and Kate needed to work out a plan for going to and leaving the office if they were going to keep his stay at her place off the radar at work.

Jon knocked on the apartment door, even though Kate had given him her key card.

The locks clicked and she opened the door. "Didn't the card work?"

He shrugged. "I didn't want to disturb your privacy by just letting myself in. I smell the pizza," he said to redirect the conversation and the uneasiness that had returned when he'd walked in.

"It has. Piping hot," she said, motioning to the kitchen bar and the delivery boxes next to the plates she'd gotten out

Who said *piping* hot, besides TV commercials? He relaxed, realizing that Kate might feel as awkward with their situation as he did. He couldn't help thinking that was a good sign.

Jon loaded his plate with a slice of pizza and several wings. "On my way up, I was thinking that we need a plan for keeping my stay discreet." He didn't see any reason for mentioning the coworker he'd almost run into at the gym.

"Me too," Kate said between bites. "Here's what I've come up with. I usually walk to work and arrive first, and you take the subway or a ride share. I'll leave my usual time, and you can time your departure to either take the subway or walk and get to the office at your usual time. The same for returning."

"I like it simple, foolproof." The later being something he might find valuable considering what his attraction to Kate was doing to his mental capabilities.

"Want to watch a movie or do you usually read or something after supper?" he asked as he and Kate finished up washing and drying their few dishes.

"Actually, I've been catching up with *Midsomer Murders* on Netflix. They last about as long as a movie.

"I'm game." He eyed the loveseat. One of the cats—he couldn't tell them apart—had left her perch on the furniture back and was curled up at one end of the loveseat. Jon sat at the other end while Kate stopped to pick up the remote from a side table. He waited to see if Kate would move the cat after she switched on the TV. Juvenile, but what could he say?

Kate left the cat where she was and sat next to him, his greater weight causing the cushion to dip under him and Kate to slide close. Or had she chosen to cozy up to him? Jon watched the program opening, aware of Kate's closeness. But rather than send his nerves into high alert as her touch often did, her side against his felt comfortable, right. Even if he didn't enjoy the show, he could enjoy being with her, watching it.

Halfway through the program, Kate leaned her head against his shoulder and toward the end, she dozed off a couple of time. He took those opportunities to drink in her delicate features and soft dark hair that his fingers begged to run themselves through.

At the end of the program Kate stood up and yawned. "Excuse me. I'm going to turn in. Let me get sheets and make up the pullout for you."

Jon rose. "Get the sheets. I can put them on."

Kate went to her room and returned with a stack of bedding that she placed on the arm of the loveseat. "Well, um, goodnight."

He pinned her gaze with his. "Not so fast." Jon took her hand and tugged her to him, lowering his head to her upturned face. His lips brushed hers and Kate closed the small distance between them, wrapping her hands around his waist. Jon lifted his hand and cradled her head to deepen the kiss and better taste her sweetness, his fingers weaving into her hair. He didn't know how long they stayed entwined in their own world before one of the cats rubbed against his legs and pulled him and Kate out of the embrace with her plaintive meow.

What he did know was that kissing Kate goodnight felt as natural and necessary as breathing.

CHAPTER 13

"See you at work." Kate stopped by the kitchen bar and kissed Jon on the cheek on her way out Wednesday morning. A more affectionate goodbye was likely to put them off their carefully choreographed schedule.

Jon swallowed his mouthful of coffee and squeezed her hand. "Yep, see you there."

Buoyed by her great mood, Kate made the walk to work in what might have been record time. She sat at her desk, kicked off her walking shoes, and slipped on her heels. It had only been three days since the fire, but in that time, she and Jon had fallen into a rhythm that she could see turning into something long-term. She corrected herself. Something long-term once she'd gotten her fund manager position, which if she could believe the office grapevine, could be this week.

She skimmed through her office emails. *Yes!* An email from HR notifying her, and she assumed the other people vying for the job, that a decision should be made by end of day today. She glanced over her shoulder across the walkway to Jon's cubicle, her first thought was to share the email information with him. She was letting herself get in too deep too soon. *Career first,* she chanted in her head, then lo ... personal life. Neither of them had said the L-word yet. Her heart skipped a beat at the realization. She loved Jon and felt loved when she was with him.

"Tough problem?" Jon stood at her cubicle door.

"You might say that."

"Can I help?"

Yes. "No, I have to figure this one out myself."

Jon tilted his head as if he was going to say something, but he didn't.

And that was what she wanted, wasn't it? To be an independent career woman who relied on herself, didn't need help from a man.

"Okay, I'll get to my work."

Kate checked her email again quickly before she dug into the analysis she'd started yesterday.

A short while later, Jon was at her cubicle again. How was she supposed to get any work done?

"Yes?" she asked.

"I got an email to go over to HR, and Grandpa texted me. The house is cleared for us to move back in this afternoon. So, you'll have your place back to yourself tonight."

But what if she didn't want it back to herself, her bold heart asked, before an unsettling thought usurped her brain's attention. Kate stood and glanced around the outside of cubicle for any coworkers in the walkway.

"Sorry."

Jon must have realized his mistake.

"It's okay. No one could have heard you. Go see what HR wants."

"Right, boss." Jon left.

Normally, Kate would have laughed at that. But her nerves were too jumpy. Everything she'd been working so hard toward could come to fruition today. And she hadn't told Jon about *her* email from HR. Maybe she'd have even more exciting news when he got back. She went back to her analysis and blanked everything else from her mind until she'd completed it and sent the information to the Growth and Income Fund Manager. The manager she hoped to hear that she would be replacing.

She pushed away from the computer, rose, and rubbed the kinks out of her neck. The analysis had taken longer than she'd expected. And Jon still wasn't back from HR. They must be talking to him about the remote back-office work he wanted. On Monday, she'd received the standard employee evaluation form for subordinate employees who were seeking another position with the firm and given Jon a truthfully glowing recommendation. If they both got the positions, she and Jon would have to celebrate. If not tonight, then Friday. And she could celebrate with the No Brides Club tomorrow evening. So far, it looked like most of the members would be there.

Kate grabbed her coffee mug and walked out to the coffee maker, which half of the office seemed to have made a run for. The chatter quieted as she approached. Or so it seemed to her.

"Coming to congratulate me?" Anthony asked when she got within earshot.

Kate stopped mid-step.

"On my promotion to replace Kim as manager of the Fixed Income Fund.

Kate couldn't find any words to reply.

"You didn't get the email from HR?"

She released a pent-up breath. Anthony was jumping

the gun a little, although he had a good chance of getting one of the fund manager positions. "Sure, the one sent late yesterday about decisions being made about the fund manager positions."

One of the assistant analysts slapped Anthony on the back. "No, the one a few minutes ago, about Anthony's promotion to manager of the Fixed Income Fund."

Anthony smiled the most genuine smile she'd ever seen on his face. "You must be on your way to your meeting with HR and Bill."

Bile rose to her throat. *No*, she was here to get a cup of coffee. "Congratulations," she said offering Anthony her hand and, given the way her insides were twisting, she hoped not some gruesome parody of a smile. She got her coffee and continued past the coffee area toward HR, planning to circle back to her cubicle another way that didn't go past the crowd at the coffeemaker.

"Kate."

She almost walked right into Jon.

"I'm glad I caught you before your meeting," he said.

Everyone thought she had a meeting. Everyone but her.

"Dottie just called me. She's taken Grandpa to the emergency room and it looks like they are going to admit him. If they do, I'm going to leave and go to the hospital."

Just like that. No, if it's okay. Kate shook her head at her callousness. What was wrong with her? She knew how much Jon's grandfather meant to him. Neither one of them had anything to do with her agitation.

"Sure, take whatever time you need. I hope he's all right."

"Thanks. I'll talk to you later. And your meeting. You've got this."

Kate waited until Jon was out of sight and checked her

work email on her phone. Jon was a lot more confident than she was. There was nothing new from Bill or HR. What if Jon was still here when she got back to her cubicle? He'd know that she hadn't had a meeting and hadn't been straight with him. Her phone pinged. A text from Jon.

They're admitting Grandpa. Talk with you later.

Kate's heart was with Jon. She returned to her work space, not caring who might notice the briefness of her nonexistent meeting.

By 4 pm and no meeting email, Kate was practically jumping out of her chair at every miscellaneous sound and getting no work done. Just as she'd decided to call it a day, a mail alert flashed on her computer screen. From HR. She held her breath and clicked it open, her gaze going to the subject line: New Growth and Income Fund Manager Named. But she hadn't had her meeting. Her gaze dropped to the body of the email. That was because the new manager wasn't her.

Kate's stomach hollowed out. She never should have waivered on her No Brides vow and lost her career focus. Never should have let Jon kidnap her heart. They'd hired someone from outside of DeBakker. Her vision blurred as she tried to read the rest of the email and gave up. Kate took a deep breath and shoved her chair away from the computer desk. She had a right to know why she hadn't gotten the position Bill had indicated was hers this time.

Eyes focused straight ahead to avoid any looks from her coworkers, Kate walked as calmly as she could to Bill's office and knocked on the door.

"Come in," Bill said, adding. "I expected you," when she opened the door.

"And I expect an explanation."

"Please sit." Bill tapped the pen in his hand on the desk, releasing it when he realized what he was doing.

"You've known, since his appearance at our group meeting that David DeBakker wanted Jon for the position."

"That's what Jon's meeting this morning was about? Not about off-site back-office work?"

"Yes, he turned down the fund manager position."

Kate curled her fingers around the front of her chair's armrests until the hard plastic dug into them. Jon hadn't told her that.

"You'd been next on the short list, until recently."

"And then what?" Considering the anger fighting to explode in her, the question came out surprisingly detached sounding.

Bill rubbed the back of his neck. "Reports to HR about you having a relationship with Jon."

Kate's backbone went ramrod straight. "From whom?" It couldn't have been Kim. "Anthony?" He'd seemed sincere earlier in his assumption that she'd gotten the other fund manager position.

"You know I can't say. Except I'll give you ..." Bill looked past, rather than at, her. "Not Anthony." He cleared his throat. "Company policy is clear. In these #*Me, too* times, the company can't be too careful."

Kate pressed her lips together. Bill couldn't be insinuating that Jon filed a claim. *No*, that was too crazy. But all of this was too crazy.

"... wants you to take the rest of the week off."

"What, wait. I missed the beginning of that." She masked her disgust with herself. Now wasn't the time to appear ditzy.

Bill frowned. "HR wants you to take the rest of the week off to think about your future at DeBakker,"

"You, they want me to resign?"

"I didn't say that, Kate. Take the next two days, paid, and the weekend to think about your position, what you want to be doing."

"I will." She rose and left Bill's office so filled with disappointment and anger that her legs trembled beneath her.

Her steps grew firmer as she approached her cubicle. She changed into her walking shoes and grabbed her bag. Bill was right about one thing. She did need to think about her future.

Think hard.

JON SHOULD HAVE KNOWN something was really off when Kate answered his phone call with a clipped *Hello*. He'd expected excitement.

"Hey," he replied.

The phone went quiet for so long, he wondered if they'd lost their connection, until he heard background noise.

"Grandpa's okay." Jon broke the silence. "Home with a written clean bill of health to send my parents to get them to back off on the pressure to have Grandpa sell the farm."

"That's good." Kate paused. "I have something ... a lot to tell you."

There wasn't an ounce of animation in her voice.

"I didn't get the Growth and Income Fund Manager position."

"What? I turned it down flat, figuring you were next in line."

"I had been. It doesn't matter. I didn't get the promotion because of us."

"Us?"

Kate sighed. "Yes, because of us. We weren't discreet enough. HR has given me the next two days off to think about my actions in terms of company policy and my future with DeBakker."

A chill went through Jon. Not only was there no animation in Kate's voice, but he couldn't detect any anger, either. It was totally flat.

"You don't need them." He took care of supplying the anger for her.

"Not long-term, but I do until I find another position. I've thought this out and come to a decision."

Jon's stomach knotted without even hearing her decision.

"If I were a different person, I could imagine falling in love with you."

The knot tightened. "Kate, you don't have to decide anything this minute."

"I know I don't. I already have. We can't see each other outside of work anymore."

He strained to hear a break, any regret in her voice. "Until I leave DeBakker."

"No, not at all. I need to focus on my career. It's who I am."

"Kate, no, you're so much more."

"This isn't easy. Let me finish. I let my feelings for you get in the way of my career, and now I'm paying."

"And making me pay, too. I thought I was in love with you."

Kate made a strangled noise.

"But I don't even know you."

"Jon, please. It's my fault for thinking I could have it all. I didn't mean to hurt you."

"As if your choosing your job over having anything to do

with me wouldn't hurt?" He wanted to rage at her, but he was too drained. "But I get it. And you shouldn't have any problem avoiding me outside of or in the office. On Monday, I'm starting my new remote back-office position."

Jon clicked off, which he knew was childish. But Kate's words had cut deep, to the bone of his childhood. For more than half his life, he'd lived with the pain of his parents caring more for their work than for him. He'd gotten past it. He wasn't going to live it again with Kate.

So why was he still holding his cell phone, waiting for Kate to call back? Jon jammed the phone into his jeans pocket. Because he wanted it all to be a bad dream. He punched the pillow on his bed and went downstairs to see if Dottie was still there. He had to do something physical to defuse the bomb of emotions that threatened to explode inside him. It was too late to hit the pool and swim it off. If Dottie could stay with his grandfather, he'd make due with a run.

The next morning, Jon jogged from the subway station toward the DeBakker offices. He was late. Not that it had any consequence in the greater scheme of things. Kate wouldn't be there to notice. A stitch in his side slowed him to a fast walk for the rest of the distance. The run last night had worked off some of his aggression, although not enough for him to get much sleep. So he'd left the house super early and gotten in 45 minutes of laps at the Culinary Art Institute's pool before coming to work.

Jon stepped out of the office building stairwell to an empty hall and hoped he could slip into his cubicle without having to talk with anyone. He only had to get through two days of sitting across from Kate's empty cubicle, minding his own business. Five steps down the hall, the elevator doors opened and closed behind him.

"Jon, wait up."

He stifled a curse and waited for Anthony to catch up to him.

"Sucks about Kate," Anthony said.

How could Anthony know about him and Kate? The office grapevine was pervasive, but the only way Anthony could know about his and Kate's breakup was if one of them had told him.

"When I got the Fixed Income Fund spot, I thought Kate had the Grown and Income one for sure. Bet she's ticked."

That was putting it mildly. "You're not the one who filed the report with HR, are you?"

Confusion spread across Anthony's face. "About you and her? That's why she lost the promotion?"

Jon could have bit his tongue off. Now he was feeding the grapevine.

Anthony lifted his hands in mock surrender. "Not me. I'd put my bet on Gregg. Kate shot him down a couple years ago using the company policy on dating."

"Gregg's married," Jon said.

Anthony gave him a look of disbelief.

"Right. When does that stop some guys?"

"And Gregg said something the other day about seeing the two of you at some carnival Upstate, near where he just moved. Said you looked pretty cozy, getting a cat or something. I didn't pay close attention to what he was saying."

"Close enough," Jon muttered.

"Hey, I won't repeat any of this." Anthony motioned back and forth between them.

"Thanks, and congratulations on your promotion."

The men parted ways when they entered their work area.

On his way to his cubicle, Jon went through a catalog of

tortures he'd like to subject Gregg to for what he'd done to Kate—and him. But, while any one of the tortures might make him feel better, none would improve Kate's situation here or bring them together. She'd been more than clear about cutting all connections between them.

He stopped between his desk and Kate's. All connections, except his cat. She still had his cat. He dropped his gym bag inside his cubicle. He was something else. The cat wasn't going to mend his heart or make Kate choose him over her work.

KATE NEVER SHOULD HAVE GONE BACK to DeBakker. It hadn't proven anything. In the three weeks since she'd broken things off with Jon, she'd grown to hate the job she used to love and dislike going home almost as much. Jon's cat Crimson had taken to howling every night until the cat fell asleep on the loveseat where she'd spent every night when Jon was staying at Kate's place. After a few hours sleep, Crimson would be up howling again at about four in the morning. Kate had tried to coax Crimson into joining her and Scarlet in the bedroom. But after the first night, Crimson had hidden herself behind or under furniture when she'd sensed Kate getting ready to go to bed. Kate hadn't had the energy to seek the animal out and risk Crimson's sharp claws to round her up before bed.

This morning Kate had joined Crimson on the love seat. She petted the cat. "You miss him. I know. I do, too," Kate said. Deep inside, she'd been a little surprised that he had totally taken her at her word when she'd said they had no romantic future. In her experience, he'd always been someone who didn't give up on something that he really wanted.

Her heart squeezed. "Maybe he didn't really want me."

Crimson gave a plaintive meow.

"Well, I want him," Kate said. It struck her. "I want him more than anything, more than any promotion or job could give me. At least one hundred ... no one million times more. I've been such an idiot." Scarlet joined her and Crimson on the loveseat. "What should I do, girls?"

Crimson jumped from the loveseat to the coffee table. And nudged Kate's cell phone off the table to the floor at Kate's feet.

She looked from Crimson to Scarlet, who meowed her agreement. "Just tell him, huh? But that's nowhere as easy as you two may think, and not at 4 a.m."

Kate stretched out on the loveseat with the cats and got in a couple more hours sleep before getting ready for and walking to work.

The first thing she did when she got to her cubicle was text Jon.

Crimson misses you. Can we get together and talk?

She pressed the send button. *Okay*, so not only was she an idiot, but she was a coward. But she could tell Jon that in person. Kate swallowed the lump in her throat. If he agreed to meet with her. The second thing she did was write a resignation letter and deliver it to Bill in person. It rankled that he made no attempt to talk her out of it, but seemed almost relieved.

"Kate, I'm sorry to see you go, but I think it's a good career move for you."

She stifled a giggle at the thought of what his reaction would be if she said it wasn't a career move. She knew the guys called her the ice queen behind her back. She used to take pride in the nickname. *Cool, calm, emotionless Kate. Ha!*

"You know the company policy. For security purposes, you need to turn over your laptop and keycard."

"Right here." She placed her laptop and card on his desk.

"I'll let HR know you'll be in for an exit interview."

"As soon as I have my things packed."

"You'll receive two week's salary and any vacation you have accrued next payday," Bob said, parsing out information in bits, as if he wanted to prolong the meeting. "I'm sorry about the way things turned out for you and to lose both you and Jon."

And Jon. Kate decided not to ask Bill what he meant. She'd find out from Jon.

"Good luck, and feel free to use me as a reference for any future positions you pursue."

"Thank you." After the debacle of the fund manager position and Bob's insistence all along that he supported her, she didn't have any reason to believe him. But over the years, he *had* supported her ambitions, so Kate decided to give him the benefit of the doubt.

Before she began collecting her few personal things in her cubicle, she checked her cell phone. Jon hadn't responded. He could still be doing morning chores, although she'd expect him to carry his phone with him. Kate shook her head. *No.* She would *not* entertain the possibility that he wasn't going to answer her text.

A little sadly, the personal items she'd accumulated in her work area over her nearly five years with DeBakker easily fit in the backpack she'd brought for them. Even sadder, she didn't really have any coworkers she wanted to stop and say goodbye to, especially since everyone's first question would be "where are you going?"

Kate's phone pinged while she was doing a final look around to make sure she had all of her things. She held her breath as she picked up the phone. The breath whooshed out. It was her mortgage broker, not Jon. She'd stop by the broker's office on her way home and put a hold on her mortgage application. She might need her planned down payment for living expenses while she job hunted. Although it might have seemed so a short time ago, it wouldn't be the end of the world if she lost her apartment.

By the time Kate had gotten everything done in HR and waited a half hour at the broker's office to talk with her and fill out the paperwork there, it was going on 11 a.m. She still hadn't heard anything from Jon when she hit the last block of the walk to her apartment. For an instant, she panicked. What had she done?

She'd unraveled her whole life for a man.

No, her life was already unraveling before Jon came back into it. He was the start of putting it back together.

When she got in sight of her building, Kate saw Jon pacing in front of the door. It wasn't like the doorman to allow that. He looked over at her and she froze, her feet seemingly stuck to the sidewalk. He jogged over.

"You didn't return my text," she said.

"Something as urgent as Crimson missing me, seemed to warrant my personal attendance."

"Yes, that's true." *Jon was here. Here in person.*

"We'd better go right up and fix the situation," Jon said.

The doorman opened the door for them. "Jon, Ms. Lewis."

"First name basis." Kate laughed.

"Well, yeah, I had to talk him into letting me wait here for you."

Kate let them into the apartment, and Crimson sauntered over and rubbed against Jon's legs. Kate's gaze locked with his.

"Jon."

"Kate." They spoke at once.

"Go ahead," she said, holding her heart close in case what he had to say wasn't what she had to say.

"Good. I've been practicing this all morning and don't want to mess it up. If you hadn't texted me this morning, I would have called you. I couldn't go on any longer without telling you how I feel."

She lessened the grip on her heart.

"I love you. I've loved you some since high school. But now I love you with all my heart."

Kate opened her mouth to respond, and Jon put his finger over her lips.

"I should have told you that when you broke things off. But sometimes I'm so in awe of you that I regress to adolescence."

She ran her fingertip over the faint blush that colored his cheek.

Jon took a sharp breath and continued. "I let myself think you were choosing your career over me, just like my parents. By the time I got home that day, I'd more than realized my stupidity. You are nothing like my parents. But I was afraid to push you, if you didn't feel the same. I'm sorry. I *should* have pushed."

"No apology necessary. I was as gripped in adolescence as you. On my walk home, I realized that I'd let my brother's old taunt about me being just a girl, not as good as him, and what my friends thought—this time the No Brides Club and my vow—stand between us."

She laced her fingers through his. "I do feel the same. I love you with my whole heart, more than anyone or anything.

Jon squeezed her hand.

Her heart hitched. "None of that stands between us anymore. I resigned from DeBakker this morning."

"Me, too. I never even started the back-office job. I couldn't work for a firm that treated you like DeBakker had."

"What about the fire damage? The insurance?"

He shrugged. "The damage wasn't as costly as I thought it would be. Grandpa and I refinanced the home improvement loan. We'll manage. But why are we talking finances?"

"We're math people?" Kate asked grinning.

Jon lifted her chin. "I have a better equation for us to work on. One plus one equals ..."

Before Kate's mind could click in on what Jon had said, he pressed his lips to hers in a toe-curling kiss that spoke so much love it filled her mind and everywhere else. She had no choice but to return the love with her answering kiss.

A plaintive howl from Crimson finally broke them apart but not before Kate had wrapped her arms around Jon's neck as if for dear life and he'd lifted her to his lap to deepen their mutual kisses.

"What's that, Crimson?" Jon asked.

At the hoarse rumble of his voice, Kate reluctantly scrambled off his lap.

"Yes, Crimson, I have it taken care of. Right here." Jon reached into his pocket and slid down on one knee in front of Kate. The cats flanked him.

Kate stared at the velvet box in his hand. "When?"

He laughed. "Three weeks ago. I was going to ask you when we celebrated your promotion." Jon cleared his throat. "Kate, will you do me the honor of marrying me?"

"Yes, yes, yes."

He slid the ring on her finger, and she tugged him back onto the couch.

"Now," she said, "We need to get back to that equation you mentioned. I think the answer is one, but you'd better check my work."

"Gladly." He enveloped her in his strong arms and crushed his lips to hers.

The following Thursday

JON SOMEHOW FELT as if he was preparing to face a firing squad as he walked in the Briarwood Tavern to meet Kate and her No Brides Club friends. On the train ride down to New York, Kate had texted him that all six of the members would be here tonight. Six New York City professional women, each, he assumed, as dedicated as Kate to succeeding in their career fields. And here he was, a mere man.

"Over here," Kate called and waved when he reached the rooftop.

The closer he got to the women's table, the more he felt as if they were sizing him up and he was falling short. And he hadn't stopped at the bar on the way in to grab a drink to fortify him. However, some of the guys in the bar were shooting him approving glances as the other No Brides Club members waved him over.

Kate stood when he arrived at the table and lifted her face for a kiss. He obliged with a quick peck. She touched the chair next to hers. "I ordered you a draft."

There were so many reasons he loved this woman. He sat and chugged a mouthful.

"Let me introduce you to everyone," Kate said.

He wiped his palms on his jeans and pasted a smile on his face as she went around the table, "Julie, you know, Kinsley, Rachel, Georgie, and Melody." The women greeted him, friendly enough.

"This is Jon," Kate finished.

"Nice to meet you all," he said, looking around the table at each of them again and noticing something he hadn't in the first round. Like Kate, all of the women, except Julie wore rings on their left-hand ring fingers. He burst out laughing, garnering him piercing looks from all of the women, particularly Kate.

"I think you ladies may need to come up with a new name for your group," he said.

In an almost synchronized movement, the women followed his gaze to their hands and laughed with him.

"Kate," someone said, "I think this one is a keeper."

"I *know* he's a keeper," Kate said, and for Jon everything but Kate faded into the background until a female voice called her name.

"I thought that was you. And Jon." Their former coworker Kim joined them. I was going to call you tomorrow, but in person is better. Bob emailed me that you'd left DeBakker." The older woman hesitated and looked at the No Brides Club members.

"They're close friends. They know it all," Kate said.

"Good. I want to offer you a job with the private equity

firm my husband and I are forming. Think you might be interested?

"I might be," Kate said.

Jon saw more than *might-be* interest in her eyes and waited for his stomach muscles to tighten with uncertainty. They didn't. He was thrilled for Kate. Truly, what made her happy made him happy.

"Give me your email," Kim said, "and I'll send you the details."

After Kim saved the info on her phone, she said "Now that that business is out of the way, let's see that ring."

Kate blushed as she lifted her left hand to give Kim a closer view of her engagement ring.

"It's lovely," Kim said.

"Thank you. I think so, too," Kate said.

Kim looked at Jon. "Congratulations. You're a very lucky man."

"Don't I know it."

He didn't need anyone to tell him. Jon slipped his arm around Kate's waist, content to spend the rest of his life showing Kate how lucky her love made him feel.

Read the first chapter of NO TIME FOR SURPRISES, book 6 of the No Brides Club...

"You're never going to believe what I just heard."

Julie Harrison looked from her computer monitor to the speaker, her friend and co-worker, Maureen. "What?"

"You remember those rumors about a take-over?"

Julie's stomach tightened. "Don't tell me—"

"It's true. And done. I hear the official announcement will be at two this afternoon."

She drew a deep breath. "Do you know who?"

"I hear it's Spieler Financials."

"Oh heck," Julie muttered quietly. Her head spun, and spots began to bloom at the margins of her vision.

"Hey?" Alarm laced Maureen's voice. "Are you all right? You got pale."

Julie reached for the cup of coffee next to her notepad and took a long drink. The deep, rich, warm liquid helped steady her. "I'm okay."

Maureen gave her a hard stare. "What's the problem?"

She couldn't tell her friend the whole truth, but part of it would suffice. "They won't want me."

"You're kidding me? Not want *you*? You're the best programmer here by a mile and a half."

"You mean all three of us? If you include Stan? But except for the current project, the apps are done. Anyone can maintain them."

Maureen rolled her eyes. "And who knows better than you that in this business, if you don't keep developing new things, you're sliding backward? They can't afford not to keep you. And besides, it's not like you're a salaried employee. They can't fire a contractor, can they?"

"No. They just don't buy any more software from my company or offer any more contracts."

"Their loss, then. You just go offer your applications elsewhere. With your brilliance, you'll probably have people lined up, begging you to work for them. I'm the one who's more likely to be out of a job. Mediocre programmers who can also do some bookkeeping on the side are a dime a dozen."

"But you're a very good one. And beside you know where all the skeletons are hidden."

Maureen huffed out a quick, sharp laugh. "Which would be a stronger argument if there *were* any skeletons to worry about. But, yes, I can find another job. Even if I am getting a bit long in the tooth. You can, too. I just don't want to. I like this one. I like working with you. Take me with you if you go somewhere else."

"I don't really want to change either." The words sounded forlorn, and since Julie didn't want to explain why she wasn't sure about her ability to find other work, she deliberately made her expression lighter and brighter. "This is probably all worry for nothing. We don't know what they plan."

"True that. We don't know anything for sure yet. I'd better get back to work. Probably a good idea to look busy in case the new bosses come around."

Julie nodded in agreement, though there wasn't any possibility now of concentrating on the interface for the personal transaction-logging app she'd been working on. She couldn't help wondering about her future. Her stomach churned with nausea as she headed for the ladies' room to wait it out on the bench there.

Even more than the loss of income she worried about crossing paths with Daniel Foster again. *Maybe he no longer worked for Spieler?* She could only hope. She should be completely immune to him, but the shiver that ran along her nerves when she thought about seeing him again told her it wasn't so.

She straightened her spine and stood. Whatever happened, happened. She wouldn't hide out, indulging her fear. She'd handled some really bad things already. At worst, this was just another speed bump on her career path, and she was in a much better position to negotiate it this time. She'd keep going.

At eleven-thirty an email blast went out to the entire staff, stating there would be a meeting in the break room at two that afternoon. No additional facts or explanation were included.

Her appetite for lunch had disappeared, but she forced herself to down a sandwich and an apple while acting like she was working at her desk. The time seemed to crawl toward two o'clock. Minutes felt like hours. The buzz in the office rasped at several levels higher than normal with people speculating about what was to come. At two minutes to two, she squeezed into the back of the breakroom, the largest space in the office, and took one of the last empty chairs. At the far end of the area, a group of four men and two women moved toward seats lined up behind a podium rolled in for the occasion. She recognized all but one of the group.

Frank Worth, president, and Jay Martin, head of R&D for Cummings & Worth, her current employer, spoke to the president and the chief financial officer of Spieler Financials. Her heart rate sped up though she tried to make herself relax. She'd been warned it was likely to be them. She recognized Charles Quigley, president, Kris Thomas, executive vice president, and Tom Wootton, CFO, of Spieler, but not the fourth person behind them. And then she spotted *him*. Someone moved and she got a glimpse of Daniel Foster talking to another man. Dan's tall, lean build and straight, neatly cut reddish-brown hair were unmistakable. To her, at least.

She wanted to crouch down in her seat and hide but held herself proudly upright instead. She hadn't committed the crime she'd been accused of and refused to act guilty or ashamed.

Frank Worth approached the podium and the others took their seats. "I'm sure the rumor mill has been busy this morning," he said, once everyone had quieted. "So most of you already know that Cummings & Worth will be merging with Spieler Financials effective immediately. At this time, I am stepping down and looking forward to a well-deserved retirement, but I trust that what we've build here will be in safe hands. I appreciate all the help and support I've gotten from all the employees and providers here over the years." He offered a little background about Spieler and said he hoped everyone could be absorbed into the new company, and so on. Julie gave little heed to it. Dan Foster held most of her attention.

From fifty feet away, across most of the length of the break-room, he looked good: well-groomed, well-dressed, relaxed, confident, and ridiculously attractive. His lean, square-jawed face wasn't really handsome until he smiled. Then the way his blue eyes gleamed and the dimples slashed his cheeks made him outrageously appealing. Right then, he wore a neutral expression as he surveyed the room.

Julie recognized the moment he spotted her. His posture went stiff and his gaze locked on hers. He blinked but he continued to watch her through the rest of the presentation. At the end, he shook himself as though trying to pull himself out of a dream.

She slipped out as it wrapped up and went back to the desk the company had provided for her. This time she didn't even pretend to work. *How long would it take?*

Maureen found her there a few minutes later. "What do you think? How many of us will they keep on? At least the layoff packages sound pretty generous." She paused. "I guess that doesn't apply to you."

"No. And I doubt the new owners will want me working with them."

"I still don't get that. You're Miss Super Programmer."

"Not to them."

"You sound like you know them."

"I do. I worked for the company at one time."

"Oh. Didn't know that. But it didn't end well, obviously."

"No. It didn't. But it's not something I can talk about."

"I'm sorry. I didn't know. How about the people? Can you tell us anything about them? Especially the hot-looking guy with the reddish hair?"

"Daniel Foster. He's a jerk."

Maureen stepped back. "Okay. Some personal history there, I'm guessing."

"I was engaged to him for a while. That didn't end well either."

The expected personal summons came at four forty-five as most employees prepared to leave. Julie hadn't planned to stay late, but she found herself following Frank Worth's assistant to the larger conference room. On entering, she faced all of the party from Spieler, along with Frank Worth.

The latter stood and held out a chair for her while speaking to the others. "I understand most of you already know Miss Harrison."

Charles Quigley, president of Spieler, answered in a tone so cold it threatened to freeze the water in the glasses on the table. "We're acquainted with Miss Harrison." None of them reached across to shake her hand. None said hello or even smiled. Julie refused to wilt under their hard gazes and looked at each in turn. She tried not to stare at Dan Foster any longer than any of the others.

Frank continued. "I'm told that you want to discontinue Miss Harrison's service to the company effective immediately."

Quigley leaned back and narrowed his eyes. "We did not see Miss Harrison's name on the employee roster when we were discussing this merger."

"She's not on the payroll. She works for one of our suppliers, J Varner Software. We contract with the company for developing new applications."

"That stops right now. There are other companies that can do the work."

Frank jotted a note on the pad in front of him. "May I ask a question?"

"If it's 'why' then the answer is no."

"It is *a* 'why,' but not *that* 'why'. Why did you want to buy this company in the first place?"

Quigley looked puzzled but answered. "Your company has assets that we feel could enhance our business."

"I presume you mean our suite of apps for investors?"

The man nodded.

Frank frowned at them. "Are you aware those apps were developed almost entirely by Miss Harrison? And that the two projects we have in development are also mostly created by Miss Harrison?"

The others looked astonished. Dan Foster spoke for the first time. "The ideas didn't originate with the company? You have two full-time IT employees."

"We do. One of them handles maintenance for our internal computer systems and websites. The other does work with Miss Harrison in development, but she does lower level coding and testing."

Quigley's eyes narrowed, and he glared at Worth. "Why weren't we told this?"

She suspected Frank took considerable satisfaction in saying, "No one asked."

The others looked at each other, and finally the president said, "Obviously assumptions were made that shouldn't have been." He reserved the harshest glare for his executive vice president, who was also his niece, Kris Thomas.

The woman glared back. "You gave me three days to do the personnel reviews. We didn't have time to check every supplier other than verifying their existence and looking for complaints."

Quigley didn't respond, didn't even turn to acknowledge her words. "We'll have to consider our next steps."

"Excuse me." Julie spoke up for the first time. "Frank, may I ask you a couple of questions."

He looked surprised but said, "Of course."

"Thank you. In the year and a half I've been working with your company, have you ever had any reason to think I was sharing proprietary information with anyone outside the company?"

His surprise turned to shock. "No. Most certainly not."

"And you've never had a competitor release a product similar to or the same as one I've developed before or soon after we introduced it."

"No. In fact, your ideas have put us so far ahead, only a few of our competitors are catching up even now. And at least two companies have wanted to buy us out just to get those apps you created."

"Thank you." She looked at the others, keeping most of her attention on Quigley. "The transaction-logger app is at stage two of the five specified in the contract. J Varner has been paid for stage one. Stage two is deliverable in nine days and is ahead of schedule in development. We always honor any agreements we make. No contract has yet been signed for the currencies app. Cummings & Worth, and now your company, own intellectual property rights for all content already created and handed over under the contract for the transaction-logger app. Since there has been no contract yet for the currencies app, any specs, demos, or other material related to that proposal belong to J Varner Software Company." She took a handful of business cards and set them on the table as she stood up. "My number's on there, should you wish to discuss my doing further work on those projects. If not, I'll give you the number for J Varner's attorney. You can discuss terms for ending the contract with her."

She walked out, head high and back straight, leaving a stunned silence behind.

At five-twenty, according to the clock on the wall, the office was mostly quiet. Julie trudged back to her cubicle and began packing her things. Though they'd given her a space to make testing and some of the development stages easier, she did more work from home, so she had only a few personal items to gather.

Frank Worth approached as she snapped her laptop case closed. He held out a hand to her. "I'm sorry to spring that on you without warning. I didn't know until a few hours ago that the former employer you had all the problems with was Spieler. I might not have made the deal if I had. Or at least I would have tried to warn you it was coming. I'm going to take my share of the profit from the sale and retire to Florida with my wife. But I do know your work put my company on the map and for that I'll always be grateful. Whatever happens, I hope you'll have continued success. If you should ever need a reference, call on me, please."

Her eyes stung as she fought back tears. "I think we're at least even. You took a chance on my company, a company with very little track record."

"And have been repaid a hundredfold for taking that chance."

Julie smiled. "I've been repaid pretty well, too. Those last few contracts have done lovely things for my bank balance."

Frank nodded as she hoisted the laptop bag onto her shoulder. "I'm glad it's been profitable for you as well. Good luck to you in the future. I'm sure you'll do well, though. If Spieler doesn't co-operate, take the currencies app to Julian

McCandry at Hornhurst. Drop me an email and I'll put you in touch with him."

She thanked him, gave his hand a last squeeze, and headed for the elevator lobby. Eager to get out of the building, she pressed the button three times in succession, willing the car to hurry up and get there. Behind her, the main door from the office opened and closed at the same time the elevator doors slid apart. Julie stepped on and turned around.

She found herself looking up at Daniel Foster. At a couple of inches over six feet, he was quite a bit taller than she was. His expression looked strained and anxious. A few fine lines she didn't remember being there radiated from the corners of his eyes.

She jabbed the button for the ground floor, but he reached forward and put a hand on the door to stop it when it started to close. "Julie, we need to talk." His voice was the same, deep, smooth, and mellow as dark chocolate.

"Did they designate you to cajole me into...whatever it is they want me to do?"

His lips twitched as he straightened up. "No. I mean yes. Sort of."

"You should pick one answer and stick to it." She pushed the button to close the elevator doors.

Again he reached out to stop them. "Yes, they sent me, but I want to talk to you, and it doesn't concern what happened today."

She stopped in the act of pressing the button yet again and stared at him, studying the face that once was so dear to her. There were a few changes in addition to the lines at the corners of his eyes. His cheeks were leaner, more hollowed out, and a small scar bisected his left eyebrow.

She sighed. "We don't have anything to talk about."

He put a hand on the door when she pushed the button again. "Yes, we do. We have a lot to talk about." His piercing, silvery blue eyes held her gaze.

"Okay, so maybe," she conceded. "But I can't handle it right now. Today has already held enough surprises. And I'm late for a meeting with friends."

"Will you be here tomorrow?" he asked.

"No."

"Will you talk to me if I call you?"

She hesitated before she answered. "Yes."

This time, when she pushed the button, he let the elevator doors slide closed.

Daniel Foster let his breath rush out in a long sigh as he turned back to the office door. Today had presented one shock after another and his mind reeled. He couldn't feel more flattened if a truck had rolled over him. Seeing Julie again had been a punch to the gut. Once he'd recovered from the initial astonishment, it had brought all sorts of mixed feelings to the surface, forcing him to think about things he'd buried years ago.

She still looked gorgeous, though her light brown hair had been cut shorter and her cheekbones seemed sharper. The large dark eyes still dominated her face, but her expression showed more maturity, confidence, and self-possession than she'd had back when they were together. Her clothing radiated a sophistication and elegance he didn't recall.

He returned to the conference room where Charles, Kris, and Tom Wootton waited. "She'll talk to me tomorrow," he told them.

"What do we do about this?" Charles asked.

"We can't have anything to do with her," Kris insisted. "We cut her off and we should leave it at that."

"I don't think it's that simple," Dan said. "Jake and I looked over the specs and the piece of code from the app that was the deliverable for the first stage of the contract. It's not going to be easy to duplicate the work she's likely done since. Nor do we have anyone currently on staff who is familiar enough with the system to work with it."

Quigley's expression turned harsh. "You're telling me we have to consider working with her?"

"The alternatives are abandoning the app she was working on or hiring someone else to develop it."

Kris chimed in. "Could we?"

Dan looked at them both. He supposed the level of hostility they showed made sense, given how Julie had betrayed them all, but he still wondered that three years hadn't moderated the animosity at all. "We could. But it would cost us both time and money."

"How much?"

"By the time we hired and trained someone else, and they were able to finish it, she likely will have made just enough changes in the system to circumvent intellectual property restrictions, created the app, and her company will have sold it to someone else who could market it before we did—or at best, simultaneously." He looked around. "And that doesn't even touch on the problem of supporting the existing apps she created."

"Are you suggesting we keep her on?" Kris sounded aghast at the thought.

"I'm laying out the facts as I see them," he answered. "It appears the creative advantage we were trying to acquire in buying out Cummings & Worth is mostly her. We can jettison the projects currently in development, and we'll still gain some advantage from the apps already finished and marketed. But that advantage won't last. Especially not when her company offers her products somewhere else."

Deep silence greeted that summation, a fraught silence that lasted for several moments.

"You *are* suggesting we work with her," Kris said. An acid tinge of spite laced her next words. "I don't suppose your former relationship with her has anything to do with that?"

Anger swirled inside but he kept his voice even. "That relationship has been over for three years. Why would it influence my actions today? And to the point—I wasn't the one who was charged with evaluating Cummings & Worth's resources, including the human resources."

A red flush rose in her cheeks and her eyes shot figurative daggers at him. "I think Worth deliberately hid the information about her involvement in that company she works for. I did look at it when I reviewed the suppliers, but a different name is listed as the agent for the company, and it had no complaints on file anywhere. Worth must've known she'd once worked for us and knew it might ruin his chances of pulling off the sale if we learned about her."

Quigley lifted a hand and waved it in front of everyone. "All that may or may not be so, but it's not the point now. The question is what do we do about it?"

"Something else to consider," Dan said. "We don't know if the company has other developers or if she's it. Even if they have others, she's almost certainly the best they have. And she may well be no more happy about working with us than we are with her. She indicated she'll complete the current contract. Beyond that, who knows? If we want her to do more, it's likely to cost us a lot. A lot more than this contract. And it's pricey enough."

As he watched the others react to that, he realized it gave

him a strange satisfaction. Deep down he found a hint of pride that Julie had flourished into the ace developer he'd known she could be. And she'd grown into a fighter. That might not make his job any easier, but it still gave him an unexpected, surprising satisfaction.

"Let's worry about one thing at a time." Quigley let out a sighing breath. "Dan, you'll talk to her tomorrow and feel her out about finishing the contract. That's all we're worrying about right now."

"Then we'd better be sure our security is tight," Kris Thomas said through clenched teeth, directing the words at him. "It'll all be on you if anything gets leaked again."

Want to keep reading? Head to sweetpromisepress.com/NoBrides to grab your copy now!

Six no marriage vows. Six Mr. Rights. Will a group of strong, independent women break their pledge to one another and choose love over a career?

~

NO TIME FOR LOVE BY RAINE ENGLISH

Kinsley King loves her lavish lifestyle. As one of Manhattan's top real estate brokers, she deals with power players, royalty, and the Hollywood elite. But when her favorite aunt bequests her a wildlife sanctuary in the middle of nowhere, she has a tough decision to make. Does she honor her aunt's last wish and keep the sanctuary or does she put it on the market and maintain the life she adores?

Dylan Reese can't imagine not working with animals, so when he takes over the running of an Upstate New York wildlife sanctuary, his life seems perfect. Until the owner dies and leaves the place to her spoiled niece. Will Dylan be able to take orders from a city girl who doesn't know the first thing about animals or will he swallow his pride to keep his job?

Sparks fly in this "Opposites Attract" sweet romance as Kinsley falls for the swoon-worthy sanctuary manager, causing her to rethink the no marriage vow she made with her girlfriends, while Dylan wonders how he's going to keep from losing his heart to the one woman who's sure to break it.

Get your copy at SweetPromisePress.com/NoBrides

NO TIME FOR LULLABIES BY SYDNEY LOGAN

Melody Mitchell has no time for romance or, heaven forbid, marriage. As an award-winning songwriter, she loves her life in Manhattan—far from the family she disgraced and the love she left behind. When Melody's cousin dies unexpectedly, she's determined to get through the funeral without having to confront her past. But Melody soon learns she has an even bigger problem: she's been named the guardian of her cousin's infant daughter.

Dr. Brody Myers spends his days healing the sick kids of his hometown while trying to forget Melody, the girl who broke his heart a lifetime ago. Sparks fly when the childhood sweethearts come face-to-face at her cousin's funeral. Then he learns that Melody is now the mother of one of his tiny patients—and they're staying in town for the summer.

Will Melody reconsider her vow to never wed in hopes of finding her happily ever after? Or is Brody destined to have his heart broken all over again? Fans of second chance romance will savor this sweet tale of unexpected motherhood and everlasting love.

Get your copy at SweetPromisePress.com/NoBrides

NO TIME FOR PROMISES BY LINDSAY DETWILER

At twenty-nine, Rachel Winters is determined to chase her Broadway dreams. As a member of the chorus in a popular play, she's willing to do whatever it takes to rise to fame and earn a lead role. Thus, when her director, Michael, asks her to teach a weekend acting workshop, Rachel says yes. When she falls for a charming special education teacher at the workshop, however, she'll have an important choice to make. Will she take the risk and open herself up to love, or will her dedication to her dreams outweigh what her heart wants?

Zander Riley's goal of being a professional actor died years ago when the woman of his dreams shattered his heart. At thirty-one, he's living out a new goal as a special education teacher. He loves his job and his life in Manhattan, but he can't help but feel like going home alone to his cat isn't quite fulfilling. When he chaperones a weekend trip to an acting workshop, he meets the woman to reignite his passions in more ways than one. However, he's been scorned on the road to love in major ways. Has his heart healed enough to trust another woman, or will he forever be marred by past mistakes?

As the passion intensifies in this "Love at First Sight" sweet romance, Rachel will reconsider the no marriage vow she made with her best friends in the No Brides Club, while Zander will struggle to protect his heart from a woman who has the power to break it. As they shine the spotlight on their budding relationship, the question surfaces: Will the two theater lovers set the stage for romance or tragedy, and will they cast each other in their scripts?

Get your copy at SweetPromisePress.com/NoBrides

NO TIME FOR TEMPTATION BY MONIQUE MCDONELL

Georgie Price spent her teen years as America's sweetheart - a pop princess and star of a high school-based TV romcom - but now she's moved to New York to reinvent herself as the producer and star of a successful cooking show and a serious musician. She's got no time for anything but work as she strives to prove to everyone, including herself, that she's more than the ditsy blonde she played on TV. When her apartment is flooded her childhood best-friend Liam announces he's moving to New York and he'll find the perfect place for them to live together, as roommates. Georgie has spent years keeping her feelings for Liam in check, but will so much proximity make it impossible to resist temptation?

Liam Stone has loved Georgie for as long as he can remember. He took her to the audition that changed her life because he knew at least one of them needed to escape their rundown small rural town. Since that day he's worked hard to make something of himself, so he can be worthy of Georgie. Now a successful advertising executive he's moved to New York to finally make his move with Georgie, but she's vowed to stay single, and as a member of the No Brides Club she takes that commitment very seriously.

Liam is determined to show Georgie he's not like the other guys, in all the best ways, while she tries to convince him that he's so much more than the family he was born into. Can Georgie and Liam look beyond the past to build a future together in this sweet friend to lovers romance?

Get your copy at SweetPromisePress.com/NoBrides

NO TIME FOR APOLOGIES BY JEAN C. GORDON

Kate Lewis left the family dairy farm in Western New York for NYU and fell in love with living in New York City. Now a senior analyst for a mutual fund, she's put everything but her career on hold until she's grabbed the golden ring of portfolio manager. She's been passed over twice already, so she's not letting anything get in her way—not the pang of jealousy she feels when her much younger sister announces her engagement, nor the lingering feelings of inadequacy fostered by her brother's childhood taunts of "you're just a girl." And certainly not any feelings stirred by her new assistant Jon— blast from her past, high school math nerd turned confident competitor for her dream job.

Growing up, Jon Smith felt like a square peg in a round hole. Coming from a family of physicians, he was expected to be a doctor, too. Shy, pudgy, and awkward, he rebelled and majored in mathematics in college, which he paid for himself. He also discovered competitive swimming, shed his extra weight, and grew into his features, but he still remembers being the ugly duckling Jon recently jumped off the career hamster wheel to help his grandfather manage a small beef cattle operation Upstate and teach financial planning at the local community college. He takes a job with the mutual fund company just for the summer for some extra cash to help out his grandfather. But working for Kate, his high school crush, is an added benefit.

Attraction ignites on both sides as the demands of work throw them together. A true No-Bride Club member would never fall for the man who may be here to steal her hard-earned promotion. Despite the long-buried feelings for

Kate, Jon fears she may, like his parents, love her work more than she loves him. Is Kate willing to believe Jon and break her no-bride vow for the true joy their love could bring? Is Jon ready to trust his heart and embrace the love an ugly duckling never believed he'd find?

Get your copy at SweetPromisePress.com/NoBrides

NO TIME FOR SURPRISES BY KAREN MCCULLOUGH

Three years ago rising star programmer Julie Harrison was forced to leave her job in disgrace when code from a project she was working on leaked to a rival company and all signs pointed to her as the guilty party. Worse yet, her fiancée and co-worker, Daniel Foster, believed in her guilt, and their relationship imploded as a result. Heartbroken and devastated, Julie found support in a group of friends who all decided to swear off romance and throw themselves into their careers. Through hard work, taking some chances, and a bit of luck she has become a successful freelance software developer whose work commands high prices.

Dan Foster has wondered for some time if he made a mistake when he chose to trust the evidence that Julie had leaked code to a rival, instead of believing her denials. His own ambition to become chief operating of the company made him quick to take the company's side, but reaching that goal didn't bring the fulfillment he hoped. He fears he may have made the wrong choice and paid too high a price for his success.

Julie is shocked to learn that Dan's company has bought out the group that represented her software. She isn't happy that they'll be forced to work together again. Dan recognizes that he has a second chance with her. Though the attraction is still there, Julie won't risk her heart by trusting Dan. When disaster threatens to strike again, can Dan convince her he believes in her and she can trust him to have her back this time? Can these one-time enemies recapture the love they let slip away once before?

Get your copy at SweetPromisePress.com/NoBrides

Check out our books in Kindle Unlimited at
sweetpromisepress.com/Unlimited

Pre-order upcoming series bundles to save at
sweetpromisepress.com/Shop

Join our reader discussion group, meet our authors, and
make new friends at sweetpromisepress.com/Group

Sign up for our weekly newsletter at
sweetpromisepress.com/Subscribe

And don't forget to like us on Facebook at
sweetpromisepress.com/FB

Team Macachek

Fall in love with the strong women and fearless men of the motocross circuit

(Each book is a standalone story)

Mending the Motocross Champion

(Meet teenage Jesse and Lauren)

A Team Macachek Christmas Anthology

(Three Heartwarming Stories in One)

Holiday Escape

A Team Macachek Christmas (Jesse and Lauren's Happy for Now)

Christmas Pizza to the Rescue

(Also in the Sweet Christmas Kisses 5 Bundle)

Sweet Entanglement—An Indigo Bay Sweet Romance

(Jesse and Lauren's Happy Ever After)

Upstate NY . . . where love is a little sweeter

Bachelor Father

Love Undercover

Mandy and the Mayor

Candy Kisses

Mara's Move

ABOUT THE AUTHOR

For sweet romance author Jean C. Gordon, writing is a natural extension of her love of reading. From that day in first grade when she realized t-h-e was the word the, she's been reading everything she can put her hands on. Jean and her college-sweetheart husband share a 175-year-old farmhouse in Upstate New York with their daughter and her family. Their son lives nearby.